The Level Of Desire In His Blood Climbed A Few Notches Higher.

Alarm bells were ringing in his head. Sexual attraction was usually accompanied by danger of some sort. Every girl he even pecked on the cheek was immediately investigated by the media as a future princess. There was no question of having sex with them unless the utmost secrecy was maintained. His military background helped in matters of subterfuge, but the fact remained that usually when he wanted to kiss, or sleep with, a beautiful and intriguing woman, he had to tell himself no.

On the rare occasions when the stars aligned and he managed to secure total privacy, the moment was loaded and often quite magical. He'd even managed several actual relationships over the years, and had had the good luck to adore women who'd proved utterly discreet.

And here he was again, at the moment where he knew exactly what he wanted to do—climb every mountain in order to kiss Ariella Winthrop.

It was never as easy as that.

Dear Reader,

We can all imagine what it might feel like to find yourself at the center of a media firestorm. The public is insatiably curious about "royalty," both hereditary and elected. Growing up in England, I read endless stories about who the princes—Charles and Andrew, at that time— were dating and I still remember newspaper images of a teenage Diana captured unawares with the sun shining through her skirt and revealing her shapely legs. And having your dad become president must be terrifying as well as exciting for each newly elected president's children, even those who are already adults. Suddenly you're in the limelight, whether you like it or not.

I think it's probably easier to be born into the spotlight than to have it suddenly thrust upon you. At least then you never know what you're missing in terms of privacy and seclusion. Ariella, the heroine of my book, always knew she was adopted, but is stunned by media revelations that she's the biological daughter of the newly elected president of the United States. As a party planner she's used to taking things in stride and planning for disaster. Still, the last thing she needs is a highly publicized affair with a British prince. Or so she thinks…

I hope you enjoy Simon and Ariella's story.

Best wishes,

Jennifer Lewis

JENNIFER LEWIS

AFFAIRS OF STATE

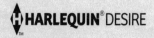

Special thanks and acknowledgment to Jennifer Lewis for her contribution to the Daughters of Power: The Capital miniseries.

Recycling programs
for this product may
not exist in your area.

ISBN-13: 978-0-373-73247-0

AFFAIRS OF STATE

Printed in U.S.A.

HARLEQUIN®
www.Harlequin.com

JENNIFER LEWIS

has been dreaming up stories for as long as she can remember and is thrilled to be able to share them with readers. She has lived on both sides of the Atlantic and worked in media and the arts before she grew bold enough to put pen to paper. She would love to hear from readers at jen@jenlewis.com. Visit her website at www.jenlewis.com.

For Charles Griemsman, editor extraordinaire, and the authors in this series who were such a pleasure to work with: Barbara Dunlop, Michelle Celmer, Robyn Grady, Rachel Bailey and Andrea Laurence.

* * *

Daughters of Power: The Capital
*In a town filled with high-stakes players,
it's these women who really rule.*

Don't miss any of the books
in this scandalous new continuity
from Harlequin Desire!

A Conflict of Interest by Barbara Dunlop
Bedroom Diplomacy by Michelle Celmer
A Wedding She'll Never Forget by Robyn Grady
No Stranger to Scandal by Rachel Bailey
A Very *Exclusive Engagement* by Andrea Laurence
Affairs of State by Jennifer Lewis

One

"The prince is staring right at you."

"Maybe he needs a refill." Ariella Winthrop sent a text requesting another round of the salmon and caviar. The gala event that Ariella had planned was a fund-raiser for a local hospital and nearly six hundred guests were milling around the ballroom. "I'll send a server his way."

"You haven't even looked at him." Her glamorous friend Francesca Crowe was an invited guest at the party. With her long dark hair in a shiny sheet down her back and her voluptuous body encased in an expensive beaded dress, Francesca fit right in with the crowd of billionaires and their buddies. It was often awkward when friends came to Ariella's events and wanted to chat and hang out while she needed to attend to the details. Luckily, Francesca was the kind of person she could be blunt with.

"I'm busy working." She responded to another text from her staff about a spill near the main entrance. "And I'm sure you're imagining things." She didn't glance up at the prince. Hopefully he wasn't still looking at her. She was starting to feel self-conscious.

"Maybe he's as intrigued as everyone else by the mysterious love child of the United States president."

"I'll pretend I didn't hear that. And I'm going off the idea of meeting President Morrow on your husband's TV network." Francesca would know she was kidding, but her heart clutched as she thought about it. Everyone was talking about her and her famous father and she'd never even met the guy.

"Go on. Look. He's gorgeous." Her friend's conspiratorial tone, and the fact that she'd ignored her comment about the TV special entirely, made Ariella glance up in spite of herself.

Her eyes locked with a tall man halfway across the room. His short-cropped dirty blond hair contrasted with his black tuxedo. A jolt of energy charged through the air as he started walking toward her. "Uh-oh, he's coming this way."

"I told you he was looking at you." Francesca smiled and stared right at him. "And he doesn't need champagne, either. Look, his glass is full."

"I wonder what's wrong." Her pulse quickened and she plastered on her most helpful smile as he approached. It was never easy to know if you should introduce yourself in these situations. She was working at the event, not attending as a guest, so was it a breach of etiquette to greet a prince? She wished her business partner, Scarlet, was here. With her background as a D.C. socialite, she knew just how to handle these dilemmas.

Before she could collect her thoughts he stood right in front of her. He held out his hand, so she shook it. His handshake was predictably firm and authoritative. "Ms. Winthrop, Simon Worth."

He knew her name? Her brain scrambled. He must have read the media stories like everyone else. "Pleased to meet you." His eyes fixed on hers with startling intensity. A dark honey color, they seemed to see right past her studied professional façade to the woman beneath.

"I'm impressed." His voice was deep, with a masculine gruffness that stirred something inside her. Oh dear. There was nothing good about being attracted to a royal guest. Still it was kind of him to compliment her.

"Oh, thank you. That's sweet of you." It wasn't often that guests thanked the party planner personally. Or even noticed that she was alive. "We do enjoy hosting these fund-raisers."

He'd let go of her hand, but his gaze still held her like a deer in a rifle sight. Humor sparkled in his golden eyes. "Not your party planning skills, though I'm sure those are impressive, too. I admire how well you've handled the blazing spotlight of press attention on your personal life."

"Oh." She felt her cheeks heat, which was unusual for her. This man was having an unsettling effect on her sanity. "I suppose it helps that I don't have much of a personal life. I'm all work all the time so they haven't found a lot to write about." Now she was babbling, which made her feel even more hot and bothered. "And it's easy to stay detached when I genuinely have no idea what they're talking about half the time."

"I know how you feel." He smiled. "I've had cameras poked in my face since before I could speak. I finally realized that if there isn't a good story, they'll just make one up and hope you play into their hands by making a fuss over it."

She smiled. "So it is better to put your hands over your ears and hope that they go away?"

"Pretty much." He had a sexy dimple in his left cheek. He was taller than she'd expected. And more strapping, too. His tuxedo stretched across broad shoulders and his elegant white shirt collar framed the sturdy neck of an athlete. "It helps if you travel a lot, then they have trouble keeping up."

"I'll have to plan more parties abroad." He was easy to talk to. Which was weird. Especially with this unsettling attraction clawing at her insides. "I did one in Paris a couple of months ago, and we have one coming up in Russia, so it should prove quite easy once I get the hang of it."

He laughed. "There you go. I travel to Africa a lot now that I'm ex-military. It's quite easy to lose photographers out in the bush."

She chuckled at the image. "What do you do in Africa?" She was genuinely curious. Surely Britain didn't have colonies there anymore?

"I run an organization called World Connect that brings technology and education to remote areas. The staff is all local so we spend a lot of time recruiting in the local villages and helping them get things off the ground."

"That must be very rewarding." Gosh, he was adorable. A prince who actually cared about something other than entertaining himself? There weren't too many of those around.

"I thought I wouldn't know what to do with myself once I left the service, but I'm busier and happier than ever. I'm hoping to drum up some donations while I'm in D.C. That's another challenge that keeps me on my toes. Perhaps you can help me with that?"

"You mean, plan a fund-raiser?" Scarlet would be thrilled if she enticed another royal onto their roster of clients. They attracted other clients the way a sparkling tiara attracted glances.

"Why not?" He'd drawn so close to her that she could almost feel his body heat. "Would you join me for tea tomorrow?"

Her brain screeched to a halt. Something about his body language told her he wanted more than tea. He had a reputation for boyish charm, and although she couldn't remember reading about any romantic scandals in the papers, the last thing she needed was to give the tabloids more fuel for their gossip furnaces. "I'm afraid I have an appointment tomorrow." She stepped backward slightly.

Instead of looking angry or annoyed, he tilted his head and smiled. "Of course. You're busy. How about breakfast? That's got to be the quietest meal for a party planner."

She swallowed. Every cell in her body was telling her to run screaming from the room. He was dangerously good-looking and must have years of experience seducing women in far less vulnerable emotional states than herself. But he was a prince, so in her line of work she couldn't afford to offend him. At least not here, in public. Planning a fund-raiser for his charity would be great for DC Affairs, so Scarlet would kill her if she turned him down. And really, what could happen during breakfast? "That sounds fine."

"My driver will pick you up at your house. It will be discreet, trust me."

"Oh." Somehow that sounded more worrying than ever. If the meeting was to be all business, why would they need discretion? But she managed a shaky smile. "My address is—"

"Don't worry. He'll find you." He gave a slight nod, like an ancient courtier, and backed away a step or two before disappearing into the crowd of well-dressed partygoers.

She wanted to sag against a wall with relief. Unfortunately she wasn't near a wall, and her phone was buzzing.

"Well, well, well." Francesca's voice startled her.

"I'd forgotten you were there."

"I could tell. You forgot to introduce me to your royal friend. Very hot. And I thought his older brother was supposed to be the good-looking one."

"His older brother is the heir to the throne."

"Just think, if the USA was a monarchy like England, you'd be next in line to the throne." Francesca looked at her thoughtfully. "Your dad is the president, and you're his only child."

"Who he didn't even know existed until a few weeks ago." She tried to stay focused on her job. "And I still haven't actually met him in person." That part was beginning to hurt more and more.

"Liam's in negotiations with the White House press office about the date for the reunion special. Ted Morrow's on board with doing it. I'm sure he wants to meet you, too." Francesca squeezed her arm gently.

"Or not. I was an accident, after all." She glanced around the room, packed with wealthy movers and shakers. "It's hardly a reunion when we've never met before. We really shouldn't be talking about this here. Someone could be listening. And I'm supposed to be working. Don't you have bigwigs to schmooze with?"

"That's my husband's department. I wish I could be a fly on the croissants tomorrow morning."

"I wish I could have found an excuse not to go." Her heart rate quickened at the thought of meeting Prince Simon for breakfast. They couldn't talk business for the entire meal. What kind of small talk did you make with a prince?

"Are you crazy? He's utterly delish."

"It would be easier if he wasn't. The last thing I need is to embark on a scandalous affair with a prince." Ariella exhaled as butterflies swirled in her stomach. "Not that he'd be at all interested, of course, but just when I think things can't get any crazier, they do."

"Um, I think someone's throwing up into the gilded lilies." She gestured discretely at a young woman in a strapless gown bending over a waist-high urn of brass blooms.

Ariella lifted her phone. "See what I mean?"

The long black Mercedes sedan parked outside her Georgetown apartment may not have had "By Appointment to His Majesty" stenciled on the outside, but it wasn't much more subtle. The uniformed chauffeur who rang the bell looked like a throwback to another era. Ariella dashed for the backseat hoping there were no photographers lurking about.

She didn't ask where they were going, and the driver didn't say a word, so she watched in surprise, then confusion, then more than a little alarm as the car took her right out of the city and into a leafy suburb. When the suburbs gave way to large horse farms she leaned forward and asked the question she should have posed before she got into the car. "Where are you taking me?"

"Sutter's Way, madam. We're nearly there." She swallowed and sat back. Sutter's Way was a beautiful old mansion, built by the Hearst family at the height of their wealth and influence. She'd seen paintings from its collection in her art history class at Georgetown University but she had no idea who owned it now.

At last the car passed through a tall wrought iron gate, crunched along a gravel driveway and pulled up in front of the elegant brick house. When she got out, her heels sank into the gravel and she brushed wrinkles from the skirt of the demure and unsexy navy dress she'd chosen for the occasion.

Simon bounded down the steps and strode toward her. "Sorry about the long drive but I thought you'd appreciate the privacy." She braced for a hug or kiss, then chastised herself when he gave her a firm handshake. Her head must be getting very large these days if she expected royalty to kiss her.

He was even better looking in an open-necked shirt and khakis. His skin was tanned and his hair looked windblown. Not that it made any difference to her. He was just a potential client, and an influential one, at that. "I am becoming paranoid about the press lately. They seem to pop out in the strangest places. I don't know what they hope they'll find me doing." *Kissing a British prince, perhaps.*

She swallowed. Her imagination seemed to be running away with her. Simon probably just wanted ideas about how to attract high rollers who would donate money to his charity.

He gestured for her to go in. "I've learned the hard way that photographers really do follow you everywhere, so it's best to try to stick with activities you don't mind seeing under a splashy headline." His grin was infectious.

"Is that why I'm afraid to even change my hairstyle?"

"Don't let them scare you. That gives them power over you and you certainly don't want that. From what I've seen, you handle them like a pro."

"Maybe it's in the blood." Her private thought flew off her tongue and almost made her halt in her tracks. Lately she'd been thinking a lot about the man who sired her. He faced the press every day with good humor and never seemed ruffled. It was so odd to think that they shared the same DNA.

"No doubt. I'm sure your father is very impressed."

"My father is…was a nice man called Dale Winthrop. He's the dad who raised me. I still can't get used to people calling President Morrow my father. If it wasn't for sleazy journalists breaking the law in search of a story, he wouldn't even know I existed."

They went into a sunlit room where an elegant and delicious-smelling breakfast was spread out on a creamy tablecloth. He pulled out her chair, which gave her an odd sensation of being…cared for. Very weird.

"Help yourself. The house is ours for now. Even the staff have been sent packing so you don't have to worry about eavesdroppers."

"That's fantastic." She reached for a scone, not sure what else to do.

"So you have the press to thank for learning about your parentage. Maybe they're not so bad after all." His honey-colored eyes shone with warmth.

"Not bad? It's been a nightmare. I was a peaceful person living a quiet life—punctuated by spectacular parties—before this whole thing exploded." She cut her scone and buttered it.

"I'm impressed that you haven't taken a big movie deal or written a tell-all exposé."

"Maybe I would tell all if I knew anything to tell." She laughed. How could a foreign prince be so easy to talk to? She felt more relaxed discussing this whole mess with Simon than with her actual friends. "The situation surprised me as much as anyone. I always knew I was adopted but I never had the slightest interest in finding my biological parents."

"How do your adoptive parents feel about all this?" He leaned forward.

Her chest contracted. "They died four years ago. A plane crash on their way to a friend's anniversary party."

She still couldn't really talk about it without getting emotional.

"I'm so sorry." Concern filled his handsome face. "Do you think they would have wanted you to get to know your birth parents?"

She frowned and stared at him. "You know what? I think they would." She sighed. "If only they were still here I could ask them for advice. My mom was a genius at knowing the right thing to do in a tricky situation. Whenever I run into a snarl at work I always ask myself what she would do."

"It sounds like a great opportunity to welcome two new parents into your life. Not to replace the ones who raised you, of course, no one could ever do that, but to help fill the gap they left behind."

His compassion touched her. And she knew his own mother had died suddenly and tragically, when he was only a boy, so he wasn't just making this stuff up. "You're sweet to think of that, but so far neither of them seems to want a relationship with me."

"You haven't met them?" He looked shocked.

She shook her head quietly. "The president's office hasn't even made an official statement about me, though they've stopped denying that I could be his daughter since the DNA test results became public." She let out a heavy sigh. "And my mother… Can I swear you to secrecy?"

"Of course." His serious expression reassured her.

"My real mother refuses to come out of hiding. She wrote to me privately, which I appreciate, but mostly to say that she wants to keep quiet about the whole situation. Weirdly enough, she lives in Ireland now."

"Does she?" He brightened. "You'll have to come to our side of the Atlantic for a visit."

"She certainly didn't invite me." Her freshly baked

scone was cooling in her fingers. Her appetite seemed to have shriveled. "And I can't say I blame her. Who'd want to be plunged into this whole mess?"

"She can hardly bow out now when she's the one who had the affair with the president in the first place. Though I suppose he wasn't the president, then."

"No, he was just a tall handsome high school senior in a letter jacket. I've seen the photos on the news like everyone else." She smiled sadly. "She told me in her letter that she kept quiet about her pregnancy because he was going off to college and she didn't want to spoil what she knew would be a brilliant career."

"She was right about his prospects, that's for sure." He poured her some fragrant coffee. "And maybe she needs time to get used to the situation. I bet she's secretly dying to meet you."

"I'm quickly learning not to have expectations about people. They're likely to be turned on their head just when I least expect it."

"You can't get paranoid, though. That doesn't help. I try to assume that everyone has the best intentions until they prove otherwise." His expression made her laugh. It suggested they often proved otherwise but he wasn't losing sleep over it.

She didn't know what to think about Simon's intentions. She had a strong feeling that he didn't invite her here to plan a party, but there was no way she could come out and ask him. Maybe he really did just want to give her a pep talk on how to deal with her unwelcome celebrity.

"So I should try to approach everyone as a potential new friend, even if they're trying to take a picture of me buying bagels in the supermarket?"

"If you can. At the very least they won't get a really bad picture of you and you won't get in trouble for smash-

ing their camera." He managed to be mischievous and
deeply serious at the same time, which was doing something strange to her insides.

"Ever since your older brother got married the papers
keep speculating about your love life, but I haven't seen
any stories about it. How do you keep your personal life
out of the papers?" Uh-oh, now she was asking him about
his love life, in a roundabout way. She regretted the question, but also burned with curiosity to see how he'd answer. Was he involved with anyone?

"I have privacy." He gestured at their elegant surroundings. "I just have to be cunning to get it." His eyes shone.
They were the color of neat whiskey, and were starting to
have a similarly intoxicating effect on her. He had a light
stubble on his cheeks, not dark, but enough to add texture
under his cheekbones and she wondered what it would
feel like to touch it. This was the private Simon the public
didn't see, and he'd invited her into his exclusive world.

Her breathing had quickened and she realized she was
still holding her uneaten scone in her hand. She put it down
and had a sip of orange juice instead. That had the bracing
effect she needed. "I guess I need to get more cunning,
too. It must help to have friends with large estates." She
smiled. "It looks like it has a beautiful garden."

"Do you want to see it? I can tell you're not exactly
ravenous."

"I'd love a walk." Adrenaline and relief surged through
her. Anything to dissipate the nervous tension building in
her muscles. "Maybe I'll be hungrier after some fresh air."

"I already went for a run this morning. Just me and two
Secret Service agents pounding the picturesque streets."
He stood and helped pull out her chair as she stood. Again
she was touched by his thoughtfulness. She'd expect a
prince to be more…supercilious.

"Where are the agents now?"

"Outside, checking the perimeter. They'll keep a discreet distance from us."

"Oh." She glanced around, half expecting to see one lurking in the corner. Simon opened a pair of French doors and they stepped out onto a slate patio with a view over a formal rose garden. The heady scent of rose petals filled the air. "You picked the perfect time to invite me here. They're all in bloom."

"It's June. The magic moment."

He smiled and they walked down some wide steps to the borders of roses. They were the fragrant heirloom roses, with soft white, delicate yellow and big fluffy pale pink heads, so different from the gaudy unscented blooms she sometimes dealt with for parties. She drank in their scent and felt her blood pressure drop. "How gorgeous. It must take an army of gardeners to keep them so perfect."

"No doubt."

She glanced up at him, instantly reminded of how tall he was. Six-two, at least. His broad shoulders strained against the cloth of his shirt as he bent over a spray of double pink blossoms. He pulled something from his pocket and snipped off a stem, then stripped the thorns.

"You carry a knife?"

"Boy Scout training." He offered her the posy. Their fingers brushed and she felt a sizzle of energy pass between them before she accepted it and buried her nose in it. How could she be attracted to a British prince, of all people? Wasn't her life crazy and embarrassing enough already? Surely she could at least develop a crush on a prince from some obscure and far-flung nation that no one had heard of, not one of her nation's closest allies.

"You're very quiet." His soft voice tickled her ear.

"Thinking too much, as usual." She looked up. The

morning sun played on the hard planes of his face and illuminated the golden sparkle of her eyes.

"That's not always a good idea." A smile tugged at the corner of his mouth. "Maybe we'd better keep walking." His hand touched the base of her spine, sending a thick shiver of arousal darting through her. Things just got worse and worse!

She walked quickly, first to lose his hand, and then to outpace her own imagination, which already toyed with the idea of kissing him.

"I think I've been working too hard lately." That must be why the simple touch of a handsome man could send her loopy.

"Then you need to take a break." He made it sound so easy.

"It's not as if I can just step off the carousel and spend a few weeks in the islands."

"Not without the entire press corps following you." His wry glance made her chuckle. "You have to be crafty about it when you're in the public eye. You don't want to be caught topless in Vegas."

She laughed aloud. "I don't think there's much danger of that. Oddly enough, I've never been there."

"No quickie weddings in your past?"

"No, thank goodness. Otherwise my former husband would probably be preparing a tell-all biography about me."

He slowed. "Is that a risk? Do you have people from your past who could reveal things you don't want to be made public?" Was he tactfully inquiring about her romantic history?

"No." She said it fast and loud. "I guess that's something to be grateful for. My past is very plain vanilla. I was a bit embarrassed by how unexciting my life has been up to this point, but now it's a huge relief."

"But a little dull." She glanced at him as he lifted a brow slightly. As if he wanted to tempt her into sin.

"Sometimes dull is good."

"Even in the party planning business?"

"Oh, yes. Believe me, dull and tasteful goes a long way, especially when there are scandals swirling like tornadoes all around you."

"Hmm. Sounds like a waste to me. If you're going to have a party you might as well make it a live one. I suppose I feel the same way about life. Sometimes it drives the family mad that I can't just plod around opening supermarkets and smashing bottles against ships, but I have to climb mountains and trek across deserts. Turning my adventures into fund-raising activities gives them an air of legitimacy, but frankly I'd be doing it anyway, simply because I enjoy it. Maybe you need an adventure." His voice brightened.

"Oh, no." Adrenaline shot through her. "No. Adventure is definitely the last thing I need. Really, I'm a dull and boring person. Happiest with a cup of herbal tea and a glossy magazine." That should stop him in his tracks. And maybe she was trying to convince herself that she wasn't experiencing a surge of excitement just from walking close to this man.

"I don't believe a word of it." He touched the small of her back again—just for a split second—as they descended a short flight of stone stairs. Again her skin prickled as if he'd touched it right through her clothes. An odd sensation was unfurling in the pit of her belly. One she hadn't felt in a very long time.

"Trust me," she pleaded, as her body threatened to succumb to far more excitement than she needed. "All I really want is my ordinary, quiet life back."

"Well." He stopped and took her hands. Her fingers tingled and her breath caught in her lungs. "That is most certainly not going to happen."

Two

It took every ounce of self-control he possessed for Simon not to press his lips to Ariella's soft pink ones. But he managed. Years of royal training, accompanied by thinly veiled threats from older members of the family, had taught him to handle these situations with his brain rather than other more primitive and enthusiastic parts of his body.

He didn't want to blow it. Scare her off. Something deep in his gut told him that Ariella Winthrop was no ordinary woman. He trusted his gut in the line of fire and on the face of a sheer cliff. It rarely steered him wrong.

Something about Ariella sent excitement coursing through him. He couldn't explain it, or even put his finger on the feeling; it was just a hunch that meeting her could change the course of his entire life.

He even managed to let go of her hands, reluctantly, and turn toward the rhododendron border as a distraction. "The reality is that your life has changed forever."

He glanced back, and was relieved to see her following closely. "Whether you like it or not, you're public property now." It made him feel close to her. They shared a bond and his years of hard experience could help her negotiate the minefield of a life lived on the pages of the daily papers.

"But I'm still the same person I've been all along. People can't expect me to suddenly welcome the entire world into my private life."

"You're not the same, though. You didn't know the president was your father, did you?"

"I was as surprised as he was. I'd never have guessed it in a million years. Now people are even saying I look like him. It seems insane to me. I don't feel in the least bit related to him."

Simon surveyed her strikingly pretty face. She had elegant, classical features, highlighted by the sparkle of warmth from her people-oriented personality. "You do look rather like him. You both have striking bone structure, and something about your eyes seems familiar."

She let out an exasperated sigh. "You're just imagining it. Or trying to make me feel better, and it's not working. Yes, I'd like to meet him, since we do share the same genes, but I'm sure I'll never have the same feelings for him as I do for the man who actually raised me."

"Of course not." He frowned. Her moss-green eyes were filled with concern. "No one expects you to do that."

"I feel like they do." she protested. "Journalists keep talking to me as if I must be happy to have President Morrow as my father. He's so popular and successful that I must be dying to claim his revered family tree as my own. I couldn't care less. I'd rather be descended from some nice man whom I could actually meet and get to know, not some almighty, carved-from-stone figure that everyone bows down to. It's exasperating."

He chuckled. "Maybe he isn't as carved in stone as you think. Sometimes people expect members of the royal family to behave like granite statues, but believe me, we have feelings, too. It can be very inconvenient." Like right now, when he longed to take this troubled and lovely woman in his arms and give her a big bear hug.

Once again he restrained himself. He'd learned to do a pretty passable impression of a granite statue when the occasion called for it.

"I don't think the press wants me to be a granite statue. I think they'd like to see me go right to pieces. The way they've been hounding me and peppering me with questions, it feels like they're just waiting for me to say the wrong thing or break down sobbing. They must be exasperated that I'm so dull I couldn't give them a good story even if I wanted to." The morning breeze whipped her dark dress against her body. The soft fabric hugged contours that would bring a weaker man to his knees. If only he wasn't a gentleman.

"You're anything but dull."

"Why are we talking about me? That's a dull topic if there ever was one." Her eyes flashed something that warned him off. "Didn't you invite me here to help you plan a party?"

He frowned. Had he used that as an excuse? He just wanted to get to know her better. It was a good idea, though. He'd like to raise awareness of World Connect in the US and gain some new donors. "Do you think you could help me put together a fund-raiser for World Connect? We've never done one on this side of the Atlantic before."

"Absolutely." Her face lit up and he could almost feel her lungs fill with relief. "We organize gala events all the time. We can pretty much print out a guest list of people who like to support worthy causes. Happily there are a lot of them in D.C."

"They sound ideal. And I wouldn't turn up my nose at people who want to donate for the tax benefits, either."

She grinned. "They're often the most generous ones. What kind of venue did you have in mind?"

He tried to look like he'd put some thought into it. "Somewhere…big." It was hard to think at all with those big green eyes staring so hopefully at him. "I'm sure you could come up with a good place."

"The Smithsonian might work. There are a lot of possibilities. I can make some phone calls once you pick a date."

"A date?" He drew in a breath. "What would you suggest?" A date far off into the future might be good, so he'd have plenty of excuses to get together with her for brainstorming and planning.

"Summers aren't ideal because a lot of people go away to the beach. I'd recommend the fall or winter. Something about the short days makes people want to get dressed up in their sparkliest outfits and stay out late."

"November or December, then. You can choose a date that works for the venue." Perfect. Five or six months of meetings with Ariella should be enough time for…

For what? What exactly did he intend to do with her?

For once he wasn't sure. All he knew is that he wanted to be close to her. To hear her voice. To touch her…

"My partner, Scarlet, keeps a master list of venues and cultivates relationships with the people who run them. We should talk to her. It's important to find out what else is going on that week, too. You don't want two similar events taking place on the same night, or even back to back."

"Of course not." He jerked back his hand, which was heading toward hers. He needed to keep himself in check or she'd send her partner to meet with him. "I'll rely entirely on your expertise. I usually raise money for our endeavors by ringing people up and asking them for money."

"Does that work well?" Humor danced in her eyes.

"Surprisingly, it does."

"That sounds a lot less expensive than throwing parties."

"But think of all the fun I miss out on. And hardly anyone in the US has heard of World Connect, so I need to get the word out."

She stopped walking. "I have an idea."

"Yes?"

"How about an outdoor concert?"

"In the dead of winter?" Was he following the conversation? He might have lost track when he just got lost in the way her navy dress hugged her hips.

"No!" She laughed. "You could do it in September or October. The weather's usually lovely then and we've pulled festivals together quicker than that. You could get a much larger and more diverse crowd and make the same money by selling more tickets."

"I love it. World Connect is about inclusion, so the more people who can come and hear about it, the better."

"If the bands are enthusiastic enough they might even perform for free, so all the profits would go to World Connect." He could see her getting excited, which had a strange effect on his own adrenaline. "A good friend of mine is a music agent so I'm sure she can hook me up with some interesting performers."

"And how about some musicians from Africa? I could talk to some friends over there and see who would be interested. Already the world is coming together. I'm so glad I convinced you to come here today." Again his fingers itched to seize hers. Again he shoved them into his pockets. They'd walked past the rhododendrons and out onto a lawn that circled around the tennis court. "I can't believe I lucked into meeting you."

"You hardly lucked into it." She shot him a teasing smile that sent heat right to his groin. "You came right up to me."

"I like to make things happen, not sit around waiting for them to happen."

"I guess that's the best way to live your life. I'm going to adopt that attitude from now on."

"Just keep on being yourself and don't worry about the press or anyone else. Don't let the bastards grind you down."

A smile tugged at her mouth. "I bet you wouldn't say that in front of the press."

"True. So more accurately, you have to be yourself, but not put every aspect on public display. I won't lie, it's a delicate balance, but I can already see that you're more than capable of doing it."

She shrugged her slim shoulders. "I don't really have any choice."

"In some ways, I think that makes it easier." He slid his arm around her shoulders, which sent a delicious sensation of warmth flooding through his torso.

He instantly regretted the rash move when she sprang forward toward a herb border. He shook his head in frustration at himself. He could see that beneath her calm and controlled demeanor she was nervous and skittish as a startled filly. It hadn't been easy to persuade her to come here and he didn't want to add to her anxiety by being yet another person who wanted a piece of her.

Her scent filled his nostrils, delicate and feminine, like their lush floral surroundings. "A garden is the perfect backdrop for you." The sunlight sparkled in her dark hair and lit up her eyes. Even the bird on a nearby tree branch seemed transfixed by her beauty, still and unblinking, head cocked.

"I don't know why. I haven't spent much time in gardens."

"You grew up in the city?"

"Nope, in a tiny town in Montana, but my parents didn't have a garden like this. It was a smooth clipped lawn with a fence and a doghouse. No camellias to bury your nose in or arbors to stand gracefully under."

"The president's from Montana, isn't he?"

"Yes, that's how the journalists found me. They went there to do a story on his childhood and decided to tap the phone of a former White House maid who lived in his town. She inadvertently revealed that my mother— his high school sweetheart—had become pregnant and never told him."

Anger surged inside him. He knew the story already. Who didn't? It had been setting headlines on fire for months. And since he was here to sign a treaty between the United States and the United Kingdom to punish those who used technology to violate other people's privacy, it was his business to know the more intimate details. "Have you been following the story in the press? Angelica Pierce, the ANS journalist who did the illegal wiretapping is going to prison, last I heard. She's expected to get a two- to five-year sentence."

"I know. Everyone seems to think I should be thrilled about it, but I feel sorry for her. It turned out that Graham Boyle, the former head of ANS, was her biological father and had denied all knowledge of her for years. I'm not sure if she was trying to impress him or ruin him with her illegal antics, but it certainly was a cry for help. I did hear that she and her father have started writing to each other now that they're both behind bars. Hopefully they'll have a better relationship once they've both served their sentences."

"Now that's a family situation that makes almost anything seem normal by comparison, even discovering that your father is president."

"I suppose you're right. And I did have a ridiculously normal childhood." The sun sparkled in her hair. She looked so fresh and pretty out in the sunlight. None of the newspaper images did her justice.

"Did you like growing up in Montana?"

"Sure. I didn't know anything different. I thought everyone could bike to the store with their dog in the handlebar basket, or fish in a river all day long on Sunday. Sometimes I miss the simple life."

"Really?" She was relaxing a little.

"Only for a moment, though." She flashed a slightly mischievous smile. "I do love the hustle and bustle of D.C. I guess when it comes right down to it, I'm a people person rather than a hiking in the wilderness person."

"Why can't you be both?"

"I suppose I could. But in the last three or four years I've been so madly busy I can barely sleep in on the weekends, let alone commune with nature."

"Time management is an important part of life in the spotlight."

"There you go again! I refuse to believe that the rest of my life will be lived in a spotlight." She hadn't tensed. She was teasing him.

He shrugged. "Who knows? Maybe the president will get voted out of office in three years and everyone will forget all about you."

"Hey, that's my dad you're talking about!"

He laughed. "See? You feel attached to him already."

"I admit I have been thinking a lot about meeting him, and my mother. I'm nervous, though."

He shrugged. "What have you got to lose?"

"What if I hate them?"

A smile tugged at his mouth. "Then you hate them. That's hardly worse than not knowing them at all."

"I wonder." She inhaled deeply, and started walking across the lawn. He kept pace with her, trying to tug his eyes from the seductive swishing movement of her slim hips beneath her dress. She swung suddenly to face him. "What if I adore them and they don't like me?"

"That'll never happen."

"How do you know?"

"Because you're the kind of daughter any parent would be thrilled to have. The universe seems to be pushing them toward you. Take a chance, live dangerously."

"That sounds like your kind of motto rather than mine." She touched the delicate red petal of a hibiscus in a tall clay pot. "My life is spent reducing the chances that something can go wrong and trying to be as cautious and well prepared as possible. I suppose that is an occupational hazard."

"Time for a change, then." He said it softly. She was so afraid of stepping outside the boundaries of the life she'd made for herself. Too worried about her reputation and the media and what the future might hold. He'd like to shift her focus to much more interesting things like the feel of their lips touching or their hands on each others' skin.

The urge to kiss her was growing stronger each second. He wasn't quite sure what would have happened if it wasn't for all the discipline he'd developed during his royal upbringing and honed in his army training. Even her thoughtful gaze was driving him half mad.

But the way she'd leaped away from him like he'd stung

her warned him to slow right down. He'd have to go very slowly and carefully with Ariella.

"Maybe you're right." Her words surprised him.

"You're going to meet them?"

"I'm scheduled to have a televised 'reunion' with my father on ANS, but I'm not as sure about my mother. She's in a trickier position than me, really. My mom abandoned me and failed to tell the man who fathered me that I existed. She has good reason to stay hidden in some ways." Her eyes flashed with emotion. "I'm sure a lot of people would criticize her choices, regardless of why she made them."

She inhaled, that mysterious expression in her eyes growing deeper. "And my father didn't even know he was a father. He's been rolling merrily through life with no ties and no responsibilities except to his constituents and his country, and now he's discovered that he had a child all along but he's missed the whole experience. I'd be pretty cheesed off if I was him."

"I wonder if they loved each other." He still wasn't entirely sure his own parents had. There were so many forces rushing them together, only to tear them apart again.

"All the salacious media stories made it sound like they did. Puppy love."

"Perhaps you can bring them back together?"

"You're worse than the *National Enquirer!* Either that or you're a hopeless romantic."

"I suspect it's the latter."

She lifted her chin, watching him. Probably deciding that his professed romanticism was simply a cunning ploy to get up her skirt. His unfortunate reputation as a ladies' man sometimes preceded him. "How come you're not in a relationship? Your brother dated the same woman his entire adult life and now they're married."

He shrugged. "I haven't been as lucky as him."

"Or maybe you've just been too busy scaling mountains." She lifted one of her delicate dark brows.

He chuckled. "That, too. There aren't too many lovely, intelligent women at the top of mountains."

"Obviously you've been scaling the wrong ones." She turned and strode off again, but this time her movement had a teasing air. She wanted him to follow her, and knew that he would.

The level of desire in his blood climbed a few notches. He followed her into a square herb garden, with gravel paths bisecting geometrical beds of fragrant lavender and sage and oregano. She bent over a tall rosemary plant and buried her nose in its needles.

Of course his attention snapped immediately to the way her dress hugged the delicious curve of her behind and the graceful way she stood on one leg and extended the other slightly behind her as she leaned forward.

Alarm bells were ringing in his head. Sexual attraction was usually accompanied by danger of some sort. Every girl he even pecked on the cheek was immediately investigated by the media as a future princess. There was no question of having sex with them unless the utmost secrecy was maintained. His military background helped in matters of subterfuge, but the fact remained that usually when he wanted to kiss—or sleep with—a beautiful and intriguing woman, he had to tell himself no.

On the rare occasions when the stars aligned and he managed to secure total privacy, the moment was loaded and often quite magical. He'd even managed several actual relationships over the years, and had had the good luck to adore women who'd proved utterly discreet.

And here he was again, at the moment where he knew exactly what he wanted to do—climb every mountain in order to kiss Ariella Winthrop.

It was never as easy as that.

"You look more relaxed." Her entire demeanor had softened.

She looked up at him with a flirtatious sparkle in her eye. "I feel much better. I'm not sure why."

"Talking to me, of course. And breathing some fresh air doesn't hurt, either. You should come visit Whist Castle. It's my home in England where I go to get away from it all." And the perfect location for a secluded tryst.

Her eyes widened. "Oh, no. I couldn't." Then she laughed. "Of course. You're just being polite. People do tell me I take everything too seriously."

"I most certainly was not being polite. It would give us plenty of time to plan the fund-raiser for World Connect. In fact I might have to insist."

"And how exactly will you do that?" She crossed her arms over her chest. Which drew attention to the way her nipples pushed against the soft fabric of her dress.

"Perhaps I'll have the palace guards bundle you into a plane. It's primitive and high-tech at the same time."

"That may work in Europe, but you can't just shove American citizens into planes. We've started wars with less provocation than that." A smile danced around the corners of her mouth.

He pressed a finger to his lips. "Hmm. I suppose you're right. And you are the daughter of the president. I'll have to resort to more cunning means. A hand-engraved invitation, perhaps."

"I'm afraid I'm the queen of hand-engraved invitations. I've probably stuffed more than a million of those into envelopes at this point. You'll need a lot more than that to impress me."

He stepped forward, uncrossed her arms and took one

of her hands. Her fingers were cool, but heated inside his. "What exactly would it take?"

Heat pulsed between them for a solid second. He watched her pupils dilate and her lips part slightly. Then she snatched her hand back and hurried down the brick path. "I'm afraid I couldn't possibly come right now. We have a lot of events going on and I'm booked almost solid."

Now she was trying to run away from him. Could she know that only made him more eager and determined? He walked slowly, knowing that to stalk any creature you need calm and patience, so you don't spook it and lose your chance altogether. "My loss. I quite understand, though. I'm sure we can plan the fund-raiser over lunches and dinners here in D.C. Speaking of which, perhaps we can get back to breakfast? I suspect those brioche are holding up well and we can fumble a fresh pot of coffee together."

"That sounds perfect."

"Where have you been? I was trying to reach you all morning." Scarlet's voice exploded out of Ariella's phone as she collapsed onto her living room sofa. She'd only just arrived home from her morning with Simon and felt very topsy-turvy. "We have to make a decision on the courses for the DiVosta dinner by four this afternoon so they can source the lobster and crab."

Ariella drew in a silent breath, glad her friend and business partner couldn't see her right now. She was flushed and her eyes were glassy with overexcitement. "I'm sorry. I got…swept away." That was the truth, at least. "I thought they decided on the stone crab."

"They want you to make the final choice."

"Then I've just made it." She sat up. Gosh, she had so much to do. "Did the tablecloths arrive from Bali yet? I keep phoning DHL and they never seem to know what I'm talking about."

"Yup, they're here. And worth the wait, as they're absolutely stunning. Maybe I'll have one turned into a dress afterward. I ordered the cases of Dom Perignon to be delivered to the venue. Their butler swears he'll lock it all up for me so it won't be drunk before the event. Hey, are you still there?"

"Um, yeah. I'm here." Her thoughts wouldn't seem to cooperate. They kept filling up with visions of Simon's handsome and deliciously determined face. Could she really not tell the person she saw every day about her royal adventure? "I just had breakfast with Simon Worth."

"Breakfast? It's nearly three." Trust Scarlet to breeze right over the part about the prince. Raised in D.C.'s most elite circles, she was hard to impress.

"We had a lot to talk about."

"Francesca told me he approached you at last night's event." She sounded intrigued. "And you do have a lot in common. Both descended from heads of state, both lost their mother tragically young and both lamentably still single. Quick, tell me everything and I'll still have time to call about the stone crabs by four."

She laughed. "There isn't that much to tell. You pretty much summed it up. Except the single part. We didn't talk about that."

"But you did kiss."

"Not even a peck." She was a little disappointed about that. She'd braced herself for a decorous kiss when his driver dropped her off—the prince had accompanied her in the backseat, where they were hidden by tinted windows— but he'd simply held her hands for a moment, looked into her eyes and said goodbye. "He wanted to give me a pep talk. I think he's going back to England later this week. He was in D.C. to sign some international pact to stop journalists from using illegal means to dig into our business."

"He must be madly in love with you."

"Are you nuts?" The idea of Simon even lusting after her did something strange to her stomach. At first she hadn't been sure, but by the time he dropped her home she was feeling some pretty heady chemistry. Unless it was all in her head. "Why would he be interested in me?"

"Because you're brilliant, beautiful and fascinating. And now that your daddy is a head of state you're eligible to be a royal bride. Wow. Just think, DC Affairs' first royal wedding! Can we have it on the White House lawn? I think everything should be silver and ivory, with little royal crests engraved on the glasses."

"Your imagination is really running away with you. Being madly in love must be messing with your mind as none of that is even the slightest bit likely to happen."

"You're right. I'd imagine Simon would need to get married in England. A royal procession in the mall down to Buckingham Palace. You in yards of lace and tulle…"

"Stop! Now. I command you." Part of her wanted to laugh. The rest was horrified by how easily Scarlet's crazy vision came to life in her head. She must be losing her mind from all the stress she was under lately.

"Regally imperious already, I see."

"I think I have enough problems in my life without starting an affair with a prince."

"I don't know." Scarlet sighed. "That's the kind of problem most women would be happy to have."

"I don't think so. Sure, the idea of living in a castle and dressing in designer clothes and eating banquets all day might sound nice…."

"Don't forget the pet unicorn."

"But the reality of being a modern royal is very dif-

ferent. It's all smiling at opening ceremonies and photographers trying to get an unflattering picture of you in
a bikini."

"Sad but true. And the queen is rather forbidding. I'm
not sure I'd want her as my in-law."

"See? Being a royal bride is too much hassle. At the
end of the president's time in office he'll go off to monitor
elections in Turkmenistan and I'll slip quietly back into obscurity and maybe get myself a friendly cat for company."
She realized she was pacing around her small apartment
like a caged lion. She forced herself to sit on the sofa again.

"Only eight years to go." She laughed suddenly. "You're
not going to believe this. Or maybe you are. This headline
just popped up on my screen: *Prince Simon to extend fund-
raising trip in D.C.* I told you he's besotted."

Ariella realized she'd sprung to her feet again. "He totally is not. He wants to plan a fund-raiser for his charity,
World Connect."

"Fabulous! I can't wait to add his name to our client
list."

"I knew you'd say that." She smiled. Then frowned. "I
mentioned doing an outdoor concert, and soon, so it'll be
a lot of work."

"Work? We love work." Scarlet sounded pleased. "Did
you talk about dates?"

"He's flexible, so we can pick a date when the perfect
venue is available. The more publicity, the better." It was
so odd to be courting publicity at work and shrinking from
it at home. "I need to go to the gym."

"Why? You're already perfect."

To work off some adrenaline so I don't burst into flames.
"It helps give me energy. And the way business is boom-
ing I need all the energy I can get."

"Well, congratulations on roping the prince into a party.

Go pump some iron, lady, and I'll see you in the office tomorrow."

In the old days, oh, six months ago, before her life exploded, she would have gone for a quiet jog around leafy Georgetown and maybe down to the Capitol. Now that reporters sniffed around her heels, she had to work up a sweat in the privacy of a high-security gym next to well-toned congresswomen and senators, just to preserve some privacy. Wearing headphones and focused on their fitness goals, they left her in peace. Something she'd had very little of lately.

And now Simon Worth had decided to stay in D.C.

Three

How did a prince ask a girl on a date? The question kept Ariella awake late that night. The days of messengers delivering quill-penned invitations were over. Did His Majesty email it? Or was a discreet phone call possible in this age of rampant wiretapping?

She cursed herself for wondering. If Simon called her again it would be a simple business meeting to plan his party. If he even still intended to do the fund-raiser. He probably wouldn't want to see her again after she'd turned down his invitation to visit him in England. Which would be perfect, since the last thing she needed was more drama in her life.

But her question was answered when he showed up on her doorstep, totally undisguised and unannounced.

"Hi." She managed, after a moment of rather stunned silence. "Would you like to come in?"

"Thank you." His tall and broad form made her eighteenth-century doorway look small.

She glanced nervously around. Thank heaven she was a neat freak and had just put away her laundry. It was Saturday around noon and she'd been trying to decide whether to spend her afternoon looking at paintings in a museum or fondling interesting objects at a flea market. Since she hadn't made up her mind (frigid air conditioning versus sticky D.C. summer humidity) she was dressed in jeans and a spaghetti-strap tank top. Not exactly what you'd don if you expected a prince to stop by.

"Your house is lovely."

"Thanks. I only have the first floor. I rent it from the couple who own the upstairs. They have a separate entrance around the side. I do like it, though." She was babbling. He was only being polite. Her tiny and rather overstuffed space must have seemed quaint and eccentric to him. "Do sit down. How did you know I'd be here?"

"I didn't." He eased himself into her cream loveseat. "Do you live alone?"

"Yes. I keep such crazy hours and really need my sleep when I finally have time for it. I tried living with roommates but it never worked out for long."

"So all of these interesting things are yours?" He picked up a pocket-size nineteenth-century brass telescope she'd scored at an estate sale in Virginia.

"I'm afraid so. You can see I love to collect interesting trinkets."

He expertly opened the piece and trained it out the window, then glanced up and his eyes met hers. Her breath stuck at the bottom of her lungs for a moment. How did he have that effect on her? She dealt with celebrities and big shots all day long and had a strict policy of treating them like the ordinary people that they were, if you ignored all those extra zeros in their bank accounts. She'd worked with royals from Sweden, Monaco and Saudi Arabia, among others, and hadn't given a second thought to their supposedly blue blood. But somehow around Simon Worth she felt lightheaded and tongue tied as a naive schoolgirl.

"I can see you have good taste. I've grown up surrounded by fine things, and never had to exert myself to acquire any. It looks as if you've done the work of three hundred years of collectors." He picked up a hand-painted miniature of a lady and her poodle.

"Isn't she sweet? A client from England gave her to me to thank me for planning her wedding in Maryland. In a way I suppose I've stolen her from among your national treasures."

"Perhaps she's simply traveling for a while." His smile melted a little piece of her. "Objects might get restless, just as people do."

She laughed. "I sometimes wonder how they feel about being bought or sold or traded to a new person. I know that inanimate objects aren't supposed to have feelings, but they must carry some energy from the people and places they've been before."

"I know places can have their own spirit. My home at Whist Castle practically bustles with it." He leaned forward, his eyes sparkling. "If places can have a feeling, why not things as well?"

"I'm glad you don't think I'm a nut. I do enjoy seeking out little treasures. In fact I was thinking of ducking past any photographers and doing that this afternoon at the Eastern Market."

"Perhaps we could go together." He said it quite calmly, as if it wasn't the most outlandish idea she'd every heard.

"But if people see us together…they might talk."

"About what?" He leaned back, face calmly pleasant.

Suddenly she felt like an idiot for suggesting that people might gossip about a romance between them. Obviously that existed only in her own mind. What would a British royal be doing with her? "I'm being paranoid again. I probably think the press cares far more about me than they actually do."

"If anyone asks, we can tell them you're helping me source interesting items for a fund-raiser we're planning." He picked a pair of tiny silver sewing scissors and snipped the air with them.

"The outdoor concert?"

"A mad hatter's tea party, perhaps?" A cute dimple appeared in his left cheek. "People do expect us Brits to be eccentric, after all. You won't actually need a reasonable explanation."

"Well, in that case, let's go."

"Is there another way out of here?" He'd risen to his feet and offered his hand to her.

"You mean, besides the front door?"

He nodded. "I'm afraid I was spotted arriving here."

"The short guy with the ponytail?"

"The very same."

"Ugh. He's freelance and has sold pictures of me to at least three different papers. One was a picture of me carrying two grocery bags, and somehow he managed to bribe the cashier into handing over my receipt so everyone could learn what brand of aspirin I prefer. And there isn't another way out. I guess you'll have to stay here forever."

Her hand heated inside his as he helped her to her feet. He didn't look at all put out by either the photographer or the prospect of spending the rest of his life in Apt. 1A.

"I do hate to assist these lowlifes in their trade. We'll leave separately so there's no picture. I'll leave first in my car, you leave five minutes later and walk around the block. I'll have a blue Mercedes meet you in front of the Mixto restaurant."

"Goodness, I feel like I'm in a James Bond film." He must have planned this. Which sent sparkles of excitement and alarm coursing through her.

"Don't worry. I have years of experience in dodging these leeches. I think of it as an entertaining challenge."

"I'm game. What should I bring?"

"Just yourself."

Simon left via the front door and she rushed to the window, where she saw him get into a waiting silver SUV, which pulled away. She took a couple of minutes to fix her hair and face, and put on a light blouse and some boots, then she headed out in the opposite direction, toward the tiny restaurant as if she was just on her way to the local deli. She didn't cast a glance at the depressing figure in his dull green jacket and faded black baseball hat, though she felt his eyes trained on her.

Simon was right. As long as they weren't seen together, there was no picture to sell. The whole world knew he was in D.C. Everyone was already tired of pictures of her leaving for work and coming back home again. No picture, no story.

A tiny ripple of triumph put a spring in her step as she rounded the corner and spotted a blue Mercedes idling double-parked halfway down the block. The car's rear door opened and she saw Simon's reassuring face. Feeling like a ninja, she climbed in, and they cruised off down the block. Her heart was pounding, and she wasn't sure if it was because of all the subterfuge, or being so close to Simon again.

"He didn't follow you."

"Nope. He rarely does. I think he's too lazy. Just snaps a couple of pictures a day and hopes a story will break so he can sell them. So far his biggest coup is the day I wore my Montana Grizzlies T-shirt. They plastered that picture all over the papers right as the story about my father was breaking, as if it was proof I was his daughter or something."

"Once you're in the public eye people read into your every move. You learn to laugh at it."

Up close like this she could see a slight haze of stubble on his jaw. She wondered what it would feel like against her cheek, and felt her breath quicken. She tugged her gaze out the window, where D.C. scrolled by. "We're going in the opposite direction from the market."

"My driver knows some antique shops in Maryland. We'll enjoy more privacy there." He leaned back against the seat, shirt stretching over his broad chest. "And I very much doubt any photographers will find us."

Was this a date? It certainly felt like one. There hadn't been any real mention of the event they were supposedly planning. And it wasn't exactly professional of him to show up on her doorstep without warning. "Do you whisk women off in cars on a regular basis?"

He shot her a sideways glance. "No, I don't."

Her chest swelled a little. So she was special? She wondered if he'd prolonged his trip to see more of her. Then chastised herself for having such a vain thought. She'd better steer this conversation in a business direction. "I told Scarlet about your plans for the fund-raiser and she's going to start work on finding the venue. How are your other fund-raising efforts going?"

"That's an abrupt change of subject." His tawny eyes glittered with humor. "And I'm forced to confess I haven't made much headway. Every time I try talking about education in Africa, people's eyes glaze over and they ask about my latest climbing expedition. I'm afraid I can never resist talking about climbing."

"You need to make your cause sexier." Uh-oh. Just saying the word caused the temperature in the car to rise a degree or two.

He cocked a brow. "Sexy? How do I do that?"

"You focus on the elements of your organization that make people feel good about themselves. For example, with breast cancer, pink ribbons make people think about triumph and recovery. That makes them want to get out their wallets a lot more than lectures about incredible new discoveries in small cell cancer treatments. For a party I'd have pink pearls and pink roses and pink champagne. They don't have anything at all to do with cancer, but they make people feel happy about embracing the cause."

Forehead furrowed, he looked intrigued. "So you think I need to rebrand my charity?"

"I don't really know enough about it. Do you have a brand or logo or imagery you use often?"

He made a wry expression. "Not at all. We simply print the name in blue on white paper. I'm beginning to see what you mean."

"So what excites you the most about what your organization does?"

He frowned for a moment and looked straight ahead, then turned to her. "Including people in the conversation about our future. Giving them access to technology that makes them part of our world and a way to be heard in it."

"That's sexy. And big technology companies are a nice target market for your fund-raising. You'd certainly be speaking their language. How about 'join the conversation' as your marketing ploy, so you're inviting everyone to be part of the future you imagine."

He stared at her. "I like the way your mind works."

She shrugged. "I brainstorm this kind of stuff all the time."

"I had no idea party planning was so involved. I thought it was all choosing napkins and printing invitations."

"That's the easy part. The hard part is making each event stand out from the thousands of others taking place during the year. In your case, people would expect a prince to have a very exclusive, private dinner, so an outdoor concert rather takes people by surprise. It also creates the sense of inclusion that your charity is all about. In addition to the event's raising money from ticket sales, it'll get people talking and that will generate additional donations and bring in people who want to help."

He still stared right at her, and she could almost hear his brain moving a million miles a minute. "Where have you been all my life?"

A smile crept across her mouth. "Read the papers. You can learn more about my past than I can even remember."

He laughed. "I know that feeling. I think we have a lot in common."

How could she feel so comfortable talking to this man from one of the great royal houses of Europe? Well, she'd never been too impressed by royalty. That probably helped in situations like this.

"That's probably why I've appeared in your life to help you cope with it."

"Destiny at work." She swallowed. Did she really believe that some mysterious workings of fate had brought her and Simon together?

No. They were simply going to spend a pleasant afternoon looking at antiques. They'd put together a fun concert that would get people talking about World Connect. Then he'd go back to England and she'd get on with whatever her life was going to be.

What about the chemistry crackling between them right now in the back of the car? What about the way her skin heated when he leaned toward her, or her stomach swirled with strange sensations when he fixed her with that thoughtful gaze?

She was going to ignore that. So was he. No one was going to do anything they might regret. They were both grownups and far too sensible for that.

What a relief.

The driver took them to a little town called Danes Mills, where he parked behind a quaint restaurant that reminded Ariella of a British pub. The entire main street appeared to be upscale antique shops, with maybe a gift shop or bookstore for variety. Simon helped her from the car while the driver held the door. It was all very formal and majestic and made her feel like a princess. Which she wasn't.

People did turn to look at them. She wasn't sure if she imagined the whispers. While she knew people thought she was pretty, she didn't have the kind of looks that demanded attention. In fact she considered herself a nondescript brunette, so she didn't usually have to worry about standing out from the crowd. People recognized Simon, though. He was tall and broad and attracted admiration without even trying. They'd probably stare at him even if he wasn't a well-known prince. Maybe they were turning to look at him for the same reasons she wanted to—because he was handsome and his smile could melt an iceberg.

In the first store they looked through some old paintings and drawings, all rather in need of restoration, and admired a painted cupboard. In the second, Ariella became entranced by a group of tiny snuff boxes. She loved to open them and find the tobacco smell still there, as if the owner had just finished the last pinch.

"Which is your favorite?"

"I'm not sure." She pressed a finger to her lips. "The silver one has such delicate engraving, and I love the colors on this enameled one. But I think I like this black one best." She picked up a shiny black box. She wasn't even sure what it was made from. Possibly something insubstantial like papier-mâché. It had a delicate painting of a girl standing under a tree that must have been painted with the world's tiniest brush.

He took it from her, which surprised her. She grew even more surprised when he handed it to the shop owner—who had to be roused from some old books he was sorting through—and paid for it. After the shopkeeper had wrapped it in tissue and deposited it in a tiny brown paper shopping bag, Simon handed it back to her. "For you."

She blinked. "I didn't mean for you to buy it."

"I know. I wanted to."

"I don't think a man has ever given me a snuff box before." She kept her voice hushed, not wanting to convey any impression of romance to the store owner.

"You can't accuse me of being clichéd, at least." That infectious smile again. She found her own mouth curving up. Surely there was no harm in the gift. It wasn't terribly expensive, just a sweet gesture. "I notice you like miniature paintings. I saw several at your flat." He opened the shop door and they stepped out into the sunlight.

"I do. A perfect world in microcosm. And just for one person at a time to look at and enjoy. Maybe it's the opposite of my parties where everyone must have a good time all at once."

"You keep giving me a new perspective on things I take for granted." He smiled. "Our driver, David, tells me there's a state park near here. What do you say we take a picnic lunch there?"

"That sounds great."

It was lucky she agreed because David had already been given orders somehow. The car was piled high with white deli bags and a newly bought cooler containing chilled drinks. She was so used to creating fairy-tale meals for other people that it was rather bizarre to have someone else pulling all the strings. All she had to do was enjoy.

David drove them into the park, past several battlefield sites, to the bank of a winding river. He spread a pretty French provincial patterned cloth—which must have been a rather expensive purchase back in Danes Mill—and unpacked the deli bags filled with gourmet salads.

Ariella settled onto the cloth and Simon poured her a sparkling glass of champagne. "I don't think I've ever been this pampered." They helped themselves to a warm tortellini salad and a crisp slaw of carrot and beetroot with a sesame seed dressing.

"You deserve it. You've been under a lot of pressure lately and it's time for you to let off some steam."

She sighed, and they sipped their champagne. Not surprisingly, it was very good. "Is your life like this every day?"

"If only." That intoxicating smile again. "My life is usually far more prosaic."

The driver had tactfully vanished, and they were all alone beside the rushing stream. Tiny yellow flowers bloomed along the banks, and the rich mossy smell of the trees and the soil soothed her frazzled nerves. "I used to wish my life would go back to normal, but if this is the new normal, I'm not complaining." She looked up at him and spoke with sudden conviction. "And I intend to meet both my birth parents." Her confidence had grown since she met Simon. "It's too big an opportunity to waste. Sure, I'm scared, but the potential reward is worth the risk."

"Fantastic. I'm glad you've come to that conclusion. I thought you would. Have you managed to make contact with your mother?"

"I wrote to her but I haven't heard back yet. It's so odd that I don't even know what she looks like. All I've seen is her high school yearbook photo from the year she got pregnant with me."

"What did she look like then?"

"Young, sweet, sort of shy. She had a terrible hairstyle. It was the 1980s after all."

He laughed. "I bet she's a lot more nervous than you are."

"She has good reason to be apprehensive. She's the only one who could be accused of doing anything wrong here. She says she didn't tell my father about me because she didn't want to prevent him from going off to college, but surely he could have made his own decisions about how to handle it. After all, if he can manage to become president of the United States, I think he could probably handle supporting a family while taking his classes."

"You're right. I'd be devastated if I got a girl pregnant and she didn't tell me."

Her eyes widened. Sometimes Simon was shockingly frank. He hadn't even looked up from his plate, and was busy munching on some arugula. "Is that something you have to worry about a lot? I mean, any child you had would be in line to the throne."

"Believe me, I've heard that over and over again since I was old enough to understand. My grandmother, the queen, would prefer that none of us date at all. If she had her own way we'd all be safely tucked away in arranged marriages by age twenty."

"Have they tried to pair you up with anyone?"

"Oh, it never stops." His eyes were smiling. "They're

constantly digging up blushing blue-blood virgins and inviting them to palace tea parties."

"But so far none of them has piqued your interest." She nibbled on a crisp green bean.

"Oh, several of them have piqued my interest." He chuckled. "But not in the way Grandmama was hoping, I'm afraid. And luckily, I haven't gotten any of them pregnant, either."

"You're shocking me."

"Why? You don't think a prince has feelings like any other man?"

"Well…" She bit her lip. "Of course I know you do, it's just…"

"You can't believe I'm talking about it out loud when I should be much more subtle and surreptitious?" He raised a brow. His dimple was showing. "My family hates how blunt I am. I can't stand beating around the bush. Heaven knows I do enough of it when I'm out in public, so in private I prefer to speak my mind. Don't be too shocked."

"I'll try not to be." She smiled. His candor was refreshing. He was so different from what she'd expected. It was disarming and intriguing and she had a hard time maintaining her own cool reserve around him.

"How did we start talking about me? I was asking about your mother. Didn't you say she lives in Ireland?"

"When she wrote to me there was an address on the inside of the letter. A post office box in Kilkenney, Ireland. She must have rented it so no one would find out where she lived. I haven't told anyone she wrote to me, except my closest friends. I told her I'd like to meet her and I'm willing to travel to Ireland if she needs me to."

"How will you do that without taking the international press corps with you?"

"I'm cunning when I need to be." She smiled mysteriously. "And it's always a good idea to do some location scouting for a big wedding, or something."

"Your profession lends itself to international travel. I'm forced by circumstance to do most of my travel in the British Commonwealth."

"The countries that were in the former empire?"

"Exactly. Lucky thing it was big and had so many interesting countries." He grinned, looking disarmingly boyish. "How did your mother end up in Ireland, anyway? I thought she was from Montana."

"I don't entirely know. I think she met an Irish man after she gave me up for adoption. Hopefully I'll find out the details once we meet."

"I'm sure she's missed you far more than you know."

She drew in a shaky breath. "I don't know. She might have other children. She didn't say. She didn't mention anything about wanting to meet me."

"She's probably nervous that you don't want to meet her. She did abandon you, after all."

"I told her in my letter that I have no hard feelings and that I had the best childhood anyone could want. I said it would mean so much to me if I could meet her."

"Has she responded?"

"Not yet." A sudden chill made her shiver. She put down her plate. "What if she doesn't?"

He smiled. "She will. I can feel it."

"Psychic, are you?" She sipped her champagne. The slight buzz it gave her was soothing, given the tense topic of conversation. "I wish I had your confidence."

"You do. You just don't know it yet." He sipped his champagne. "Let's see how cold this water is." He stood and walked to the bank, where the river rushed by only about a foot below. Before she had time to join him, he'd removed his shoes and socks, rolled up the leg of his dark slacks, and slid his feet into the water. "Cold."

"Is it really? It must be from an underground spring." The summer afternoon was downright balmy. Her own toes itched to dip into the sparkling depths. She sat on the bank next to him and slipped off her shoes. Her jeans were tight-fitting so she could barely roll them up at all, but she managed to get them above her ankles. Then she dangled her feet down the bank until the water lapped against her toes. "Ooh, that feels good."

Tentative, she slid her feet beneath the surface. The chill of the water contrasted with the warm throb of intimacy that pulsed between them, helped by the glass of champagne. Her shoulder bumped gently against his, then she felt his arm slide around her waist. It felt as natural as the cool clear water splashing against her ankles.

Now his torso almost touched hers, and they seemed to be growing closer by slow degrees. His rich masculine scent tugged at her senses. She could see the pale stubble on his chin, and the sparkle of light in his eyes—they were hazel up close—and then she couldn't see at all because her eyes shut and she found herself kissing him.

Four

The daylight dazzled unpleasantly as Simon opened his eyes. He'd had to tug himself away from kissing Ariella, and the taste of her lingered on his tongue, forbidden and delicious. She looked unbearably beautiful, sitting there on the bank, her eyes dark with desire and the forgotten cuffs of her jeans darkening in the water.

"We shouldn't have done that." Her voice was barely a whisper.

"I beg to differ." His entire body growled at him to do a lot more with this lovely woman. He let his hand wander into her long, dark hair. "Mostly because I don't think we had any choice."

"You always have a choice." One neat brow lifted slightly. He could feel her shrink back from him.

"Theoretically, I suppose. But some things are just irresistible." Her raspberry-tinted lips were among those things, and he lowered his lips toward them again. But this time she hesitated. "Simon, I really don't think this is sensible."

"Why not?"

"Uh…because your grandmother would be horrified."

"Nonsense." He stroked her hair. She stiffened slightly, as if she wanted to resist, but he saw his own desire reflected in her eyes. "I'm sure she'd adore you." He really didn't want to think about the queen right now. He didn't want to think about anyone but Ariella. He could deal with everyone else later.

Ariella shivered slightly, as anticipation rose in the air. If she didn't want to kiss him she could have leapt to her feet and darted back to the car. But she hadn't.

He waited for her to come to him, and she did. Her mouth rose to meet his and they sank deep into another sensual kiss. He was almost breathless when they finally broke again.

"Uh-oh." Her cheeks were flushed. "I couldn't help that kiss at all." She'd twisted into his embrace, and her nipples peaked against her T-shirt and the bra underneath it.

"See? Sometimes you just don't have a choice."

Desire made his thoughts spin. He certainly hadn't had enough champagne to feel this tipsy. He stroked the silky skin of her arm, wishing he could bare other parts of her. But he could still resist doing that—for now. "Sometimes you have to give in to forces more powerful than a mere human."

"You're not a mere human, you're a prince." She winked.

He loved how she seemed totally natural with him, not affected or intimidated at all. "Even royalty are subject to the whims of passion." He traced her cheekbone with his thumb. "Which can be quite inconvenient at times."

She glanced about nervously. "I hope there aren't any photographers hiding in the bushes."

"I've learned to go to places that would never occur to them. Why would a man with a large rural estate go to a popular state park?"

"Because it has this cool stream with yellow wildflowers growing along its banks." Her slender fingers touched the petals of a flower. How he'd like to feel them running over his skin, or through his hair.

"That is why I come, but they don't think like that. They expect me to go to expensive restaurants and exclusive gatherings. Of course I do that as well, it's my job, but I've become quite skilled at doing the unexpected when I'm off duty. I always have my driver study natural areas near wherever I'm traveling. A man can withstand a lot more dreary meetings around a conference table if he knows there's a bracing kayak trip waiting for him at the end of it."

"Very cunning, and keeps you fit, too."

"And sane. At least as sane as I'm going to be." He grinned. He didn't feel terribly sane right now. He wanted to do all kinds of things that weren't sensible at all, especially not when you did them with a girl who was already in the public eye and who didn't fit the queen's narrow ideas of what constituted a suitable consort.

But no one, including the queen, was going to keep him from bedding the lovely Ariella.

"I'd really better get back to D.C. I have a busy week to plan for."

Again he felt her pulling away from him. He stood and helped her to his feet. Landing a kiss on Ariella's lovely mouth was enough excitement for today. Their time together had only confirmed his intuition that she was no ordinary woman. He could pace himself and wait for the right moment to claim his prize.

"I need to do some planning myself. Now that I'm staying in D.C. a while longer I want to make sure I make the most of the opportunity." They walked back to the pretty clearing where they'd had their picnic. "I'd better think about who I want to wine and dine while I'm here—other than you, of course."

She bit her lip as they packed the remains of lunch back into the bags. He could see she still felt misgivings about their kiss. It was hard not to come on too strong with her when he wanted to throw her over his shoulder and take her back to his hotel.

Instead he helped her into the car and returned her discreetly to a location two blocks away from her apartment. From there she walked home alone, chin lifted in sweet defiance against anyone who wanted to know her business.

He sank back against the back seat of the car and let out a long breath. Ariella Winthrop. Something about her had grabbed him hard. He tried to distract himself by pulling his phone out of his pocket. He'd had it turned off all day. A message from his younger brother Henry seemed like the perfect diversion, so he punched his number.

"Are you really staying over there for another week?" His brother's incredulous voice made him smile.

"At least a week and with good reason."

"Let me guess, the reason has long legs and a toothy American smile."

Simon reached forward and closed the partition between him and the driver. "There's nothing toothy about her smile," he retorted, thinking about her lovely mouth.

"I knew it."

"You knew nothing of the sort. I'm here to raise public awareness of World Connect. I have big plans. We're going to hold an outdoor concert here in D.C."

"Nice. But let me guess—she's involved somehow."

"She might be." Was he really so predictable?

Henry laughed. "Don't let Grandma find out about it."

"Why not?" He bristled.

"She'd have a fit about you dating anyone who isn't marriage material. Remember that last lecture she gave you about it being time to settle down. She's got your wedding all planned and all you have to do is show up."

He growled. "I'm not marrying anyone."

"You'll have to sooner or later. You're next, big brother."

"Why don't you worry about your own love life, instead of mine? I suppose I'm lucky that the scandalous state of your affairs distracts attention from mine."

"That's why I need you to get married and draw the spotlight off me for a while." Henry had been photographed in compromising situations several times over the last year. "Why can't you make them all happy so I can keep on having fun?"

"That might actually be possible." He watched D.C. pass by his window. "I've met someone who could well be the one."

"You're not serious."

"Do I joke around?"

"Yes, often."

"Then you can just assume I'm jesting."

"An American girl?"

"The president's newly discovered daughter, Ariella, no less." He felt a bit sheepish using her media handle to describe her to his own brother. "She's quite something."

"Don't even think about it."

"I'm afraid it's gone well beyond thinking." He smiled as memories of their kiss heated his blood.

"Gran will need sedation. And can you imagine Uncle Derek's reaction?"

"I'll try not to." He shook his head. Their mother's brother took a keen interest in meddling in their affairs and throwing up obstacles at every turn. "If only he'd been born royal he wouldn't have to try so hard to be more royal than the rest of us."

"You do realize you can't marry an American."

"Why not? In the old days we nearly always married into royal families from other countries."

"Exactly. Married into royal families. You need a nice Swedish princess, or one from Monaco or Spain."

He shoved aside an annoying twinge of misgiving. "I'd say that the president's daughter is American royalty."

Henry laughed. "For four years, maybe eight, but I don't think our grandmother will see it that way."

"I'm sure she'll love Ariella once she meets her." Who wouldn't? And in his experience, people usually got over their prejudices once you gave them half a chance.

"Oh dear, you sound dangerously serious. And I know how bullheaded you are once you get going."

"I'm not bullheaded, I just do what I think is right."

Henry laughed. "So you do. I just hope poor Ariella knows what she's in for."

Ariella was attempting to butter toast while checking messages on her phone, when she saw seven messages in a row from Scarlet that must have come in while she was at the gym. She put down the butter knife and punched in Scarlet's number.

"You're not going to believe this." Scarlet was breathless with excitement.

"Try me." She could barely believe anything that happened to her lately. Every time she thought about that kiss, she was assaulted by a rush of starry-eyed excitement and a burst of salty regret. What had they started?

"We've been asked to put in a bid on the Duke of Buckingham's wedding. In England!"

"That's great." Her mind immediately started whirling with plans for a side-trip to Ireland to find her mother.

"Could you sound a bit more excited?"

"I am, really."

"You know how we're trying to branch out into Europe. This will be our fifth party over there. I'd say this is some kind of landmark. And now that you're intimate with royalty, we have an excellent chance of being chosen to plan the event."

"You're not going to say anything about me, are you?" Her adrenaline spiked.

"Why? Is there something going on that's secret?" Scarlet's voice grew hushed with anticipation.

Could she lie to Scarlet, her close friend and business partner? She sucked in a breath and braced herself. "I kissed him."

"Ohmygod. You kissed Prince Simon?"

The truth was out. She strode across her apartment, trying to stay calm. "I still can't believe it happened, but it did. Can I swear you to secrecy?"

"My lips are sealed. So you guys have a…a thing going?"

"I don't know what we have going, but I'm seeing him for dinner tomorrow." Already her heart fluttered with anticipation—and fear of where this would lead.

"You're dating a prince. Wow. It's a crying shame that I can't put out a PR release about it. Can you imagine how much we could raise our prices if people knew you were practically a princess?"

"Would you stop! I'm not practically anything, except late for work."

"You're totally going to London to pitch this."

"Fine. Can I eat my toast now and we'll talk when I come into the office?"

"Oh, okay. Make me wait for details. You're cruel like that. I'll see you in a few."

Ariella put the phone down and tried to distract herself by spreading some more butter. She only liked real butter but it was annoying to wait for it to melt enough to spread. She unscrewed the lid of her favorite organic apricot jam, and the phone rang again. What now? It wasn't even eight-fifteen in the morning yet.

She glanced at the number. Unavailable. Frowning, she picked up the phone. "Hello."

"Is that Ariella?" She didn't recognize the voice. It sounded very far away.

"This is Ariella."

"Oh, hello." The line crackled with static.

"Who's this?" She was growing impatient, trying to spread with one hand.

"It's your, it's…Eleanor. Eleanor Daly."

Her mother. Her breath caught in her throat and she dropped the knife with a clatter and gripped the phone tighter. "I'm so glad you called. Thank you so much for writing to me. You have no idea how much that letter meant." So many thoughts unfolded in her brain and she tried not to panic.

"The agency didn't think it was a good idea for me to contact you when you were a child. They wouldn't tell me who adopted you. I never stopped thinking about you. Never."

The emotion in her mother's voice made her chest constrict. "I've always wanted to meet you. Could we get together?" She spoke fast, afraid that at any minute the call would drop and she'd lose the fragile new connection.

"I live in Ireland."

Ariella's brain was racing, as she tried to mentally organize the long-awaited meeting with her birth mother. "I have to come to England soon for work. Would it be okay if I came to visit you in Ireland?" The words rushed out, and suddenly she was terrified Eleanor would say no.

Why did she think of her as Eleanor and not her mother? Of course she wasn't "Mom" to her. That title would always be held by the woman who'd raised her and who she still missed every day. But she wanted to meet Eleanor so much it was a dull ache inside her all the time now.

After a long pause, Eleanor spoke again. "I'm in a remote rural area. Perhaps I could come to England to visit you while you're there?"

"I'd like that very much." Exhilaration roared through her and her hands started shaking, causing her to press the phone against her ear. "I don't know the exact dates I'll be there yet. What works for you?"

"Oh, anything, really. I'm widowed now, and I do babysitting for income so I don't have any real commitments." Eleanor suddenly sounded more relaxed.

"I can't wait to meet you. It doesn't seem fair that I don't know what you look like. You can see pictures of me in the papers all the time."

She laughed. "I'm afraid I'm not very glamorous. I probably look like a typical Irish housewife. I've lived in Ireland since the year after I...had you. I haven't been back to the States since. I was trying so hard to run away from everything. From you and Ted and the mess I'd gotten myself into."

"I'm so glad you wrote to me."

"It was a hard letter to write. I knew I had to reach out

to you and I didn't know how. I was afraid. I am afraid. I know everyone thinks I made the wrong choices back then and I…" Her voice trailed off.

"You made the choices you had to make. No one blames you for them."

"There wasn't a day where I didn't think of you and wonder what you were doing right at that moment."

"I had a great childhood." She couldn't believe she was finally having this conversation she'd waited so long for.

"I'm so happy to hear that." She could hear tears in her mother's voice. "I did worry. I tried to imagine that you were being well taken care of and were happy."

"I could show you photos if you'd like. My dad was an avid photographer and there are really far too many of them." Then she wondered if she'd said the wrong thing. Would Eleanor find it painful to see all this evidence of someone else raising her child?

"I'd like that very much." Emotion heightened the pitch of her voice. "I've missed so much. I never did have another child. You're my only one."

She couldn't believe she was actually talking to her mother after all these years. So many questions flooded her mind. Things she'd always wanted to know. "Do you have brown hair?"

"I do, though I admit to coloring it now to cover some gray. And I can see you have my green eyes."

"Those are from you? People have always asked me about them. Green eyes are quite unusual. I wonder what other characteristics we share? Oh, I wish I could leave for the airport right now."

"I'm so glad I'll finally meet you after all these years. I do feel terrible guilt about what happened. That poor Ted never knew he had a beautiful daughter growing up all that time. I don't think I'll ever forgive myself for that. Have the two of you become close now?"

She hesitated. "Actually I haven't met him yet. Since he's the president he's surrounded by all sorts of high security and no one entirely believed the story that I'm his daughter until the DNA test results came out. I don't think the White House knows quite what to do with me."

She rambled on. "And I suppose he's busy running the country. And dealing with that mess in the Middle East. They're thinking of sending troops." Every time she watched the news now she felt each domestic and international event a bit more keenly, knowing that her own flesh and blood had to make decisions about how to handle each crisis.

"Oh, I just thought that since you were both in Washington…"

She shoved a hand through her hair and tried to keep her embarrassment out of her voice. "We're going to meet very soon. ANS is arranging a televised special and we're going to appear on camera together." She wanted to sound happy and excited, not terrified.

"You won't tell anyone that we're going to meet, though, right?" Eleanor's voice had shrunk again.

"I promise I won't tell a soul. Is it okay if I call you sometime?" She'd already scribbled down the number, afraid it might disappear into the recesses of her phone or get accidentally deleted.

"I'd like that very much."

They ended the phone call with much excitement about the planned meeting. Ariella then managed to wolf down the toast and dash to work before her first appointment, adrenaline pounding in her veins like a dangerous drug. The receptionist handed her a message that Francesca wanted to chat about the upcoming ANS special that would bring her together with her famous father.

"It's lucky I thrive on being busy," she muttered to herself, as she opened the door to her office. She had umpteen phone calls to make about events happening this week, and now her mind was being tugged between the prospect of meeting her mother, doing a TV show with her father and, of course, seeing Simon again. There was way too much going on for everything to work out smoothly. That was something she'd learned early on in her years as an event planner. Too many balls in the air meant broken pieces on the floor, and soon.

But which ball would crash first?

On the evening of her date with Simon she left work early so she'd have time for a shower. She was about to climb in and wash her hair when she remembered she'd run out of conditioner. Great. Frizzy hair for her dinner with a prince. She'd have to head to the deli around the corner and pick some up.

She tied up her hair and put on jeans and a jacket. There was no more running to the store in shorts and a tank top now that reporters lurked in every crevice.

She strode into the shop and picked up a bottle of some harmless-looking generic conditioner—the store didn't carry her rather esoteric favorite—and marched up to the counter, fishing in her pocket for cash. A magazine behind the counter caught her eye. *Royal Watch* was the title, emblazoned in yellow letters.

Simon's gorgeous face almost totally filled the front cover. The rest of it, unfortunately, was hogged by the shiny, overly made-up face of a young blonde woman pressing her cheek against his. A young woman who was most decidedly not Ariella Winthrop.

"Two ninety-nine." The cashier's voice tugged her back to the present.

She handed him a twenty. "And I'll take that magazine, too." Her voice came out hoarse. She pointed at *Royal Watch*. "Research for work." Because of course she was just buying it to see if there was any information about what the Duke of Buckingham might want for his wedding decorations. Yeah. That was it.

She hurried back to her apartment with the magazine rolled tightly. She certainly didn't need any press coverage of her buying *Royal Watch*. Once inside she locked the door and walked slowly to the kitchen counter, now almost afraid to look at the cover again. Was she jealous? She'd only just met Simon. He must have an entire history of romances that had nothing to do with his feelings for her.

She risked another glance at the girl on the cover. Blue eyes, heavily outlined with dark eyeliner. The text over the photo said *Prince Simon Engaged!*

She frowned. He couldn't be in love with someone else and kissing her—could he? She flipped to the "article," which consisted of two paragraphs accompanied by a lot more pictures. All the photos appeared to be from the same outdoor sporting event—some kind of horse race—with all the women in big hats.

The article said that Lady Sophia Alnwick and Prince Simon had told their closest friends of their planned engagement, and that the queen was thrilled to welcome her new daughter-in-law into the family.

How come she hadn't seen any of this in the more mainstream press? Prince Simon wasn't as much in the public eye as his older brother, who was heir to the throne, but the entertainment press still picked up on stories about him quite often. Could *Royal Watch* simply have made it up?

Apart from the cover picture where they appeared to be cheek to cheek, they didn't look that intimate. Still…

She showered and dressed with considerably less excitement and more trepidation than she'd been feeling before she saw *Royal Watch*. How could she bring this up without seeming like a jealous harpy? On the other hand, she certainly didn't want to kiss a man who was engaged—even unofficially—to another woman.

When Simon's driver opened the rear door of the car thirty minutes later, she was surprised to find it empty. Did she now expect one of the crowned heads of Europe to arrive in person to pick her up? She was definitely getting a big head.

The car slid through the more exclusive streets of the city. She had no idea where they were going, but somehow it seemed embarrassing to admit it to the driver, so she didn't ask. Before long, they pulled up in front of a classical façade. The driver opened the door and she stepped out. The building looked grand and impersonal, like an embassy or an exclusive law office. She walked up the front steps and a suited man opened the door and murmured "Good evening." Still no sign of Simon. If her life wasn't so unpredictable and over the top already she'd probably be growing alarmed by now.

"Ariella." His deep, smooth voice called from down a marbled hallway. Immediately her body heat rose.

He walked up to her and kissed her softly on the lips. *Who's Sophia Alnwick?* she wanted to ask, but now was not the time. Her mouth hummed under his kiss and she wanted it to deepen, but the man who'd opened the door must be nearby, and maybe others, too. She didn't want anyone to find out about their clandestine affair.

An affair? That sounded so…sexual. And it wasn't. At least not yet.

"What is this place?"

"An unofficial annex to the consulate. There's no one here in the evenings so I've requisitioned it so I could entertain you *at home,* so to speak. We'll just have to pretend we're at Whist Castle, since you won't do me the honor of visiting me at my real home."

His teasing hurt expression made her laugh. He always managed to diffuse any tension in the situation and make her feel like they were just two people who happened to get along well. "As it turns out, I might be planning a party in England soon."

He picked up her hand and kissed it, which made her fingers tingle with pleasure. "Then perhaps I'll have some beefeaters intercept you and whisk you up to Whist." His eyes glimmered with humor.

"You wouldn't."

"Wouldn't I?" One brow rose as if he was asking the question of himself. "You don't ever really know what you'll do in any given situation until you're faced with it. That's something I learned during my time in the military. You can only hope you'll do what you know is right."

"Speaking of which, are you engaged?" There, it was out. And ringing boldly through the marble-clad hallway. Any staff who were lingering in the corners had just seen them kiss, making the question really embarrassing.

"Engaged as in busy?" He gestured for her to enter a room.

Which she did, glad to get out of the echoing hallway. They were now in a large sitting room, with damask curtains and big armchairs. "Engaged as in betrothed." She managed to stay fairly calm while she waited for his response. Was he going to deny it?

"Most definitely not."

He did deny it. "I saw a cover story about it in a magazine in my local deli."

He didn't look the slightest bit flustered. "Do you believe everything you read in the papers?"

Her face heated slightly. "No. Especially not if it's written about me." She felt a smile creeping across her mouth. "I should have known it wasn't true."

"But you had to ask anyway." His gaze challenged her.

"Yes." She lifted her chin. "I don't kiss men who belong to someone else."

"I'm relieved to hear it. And I love the way you came right out and asked. I get so tired of people beating about the bush. You're a breath of fresh air."

"I'm not sure how fresh I am. I've had a rather long day. I just learned that the Saudi prince whose wedding we're planning for next month requires that the men and the women celebrate in different rooms."

"We princes can be quite high-maintenance." His cute dimple appeared. "Though that does rather seem like it would take the fun out of the occasion."

"So the queen isn't thrilled that you're to wed Sophia Alnwick, as the magazine proclaimed."

He shrugged. "I suspect the queen would be more than thrilled if I was to wed Sophia. I, on the other hand, feel differently."

She giggled. She loved his dry humor. "So the palace is trying to set you up with her because she's suitable royal bride material."

"Yup." He sighed. "Blood as blue as a robin's egg, pretty as an English rose and not terribly bright. All the makings of a royal bride."

"But not your cup of tea."

"I prefer women with keen intelligence, even if that

makes them more troublesome." A smile tugged at the corner of his mouth.

"I can't be that intelligent or I wouldn't be spending time with you when I'm trying to avoid media attention. I think you might be the most eligible bachelor in the known world."

"You'd think they could find something more compelling to write about. Global warming, for example."

"Nah. Too serious. Handsome princes are more fun to read about. Especially when they're kissing the wrong woman."

He'd closed the door and now stood in front of her. His expression was serious, brows lowered and eyes thoughtful. "I'd much rather be kissing the right woman."

Uh-oh. An inner warning signal flashed inside Ariella. *Getting in too deep.* His steady gaze held her like a vise. She could feel her breathing quicken and her body heat rise. Her mouth itched to kiss him and her fingers to sink into his shirt. Isn't that why she'd come here?

His gaze lowered to her lips, which quivered with awareness.

Where was this going? This was obviously some kind of vacation fling for Simon and he'd fly back to England and be dating English roses again before the end of the month. She didn't usually embark on any kind of relationship unless she saw some kind of future in it, which might explain why she was usually free to work events on Saturday nights.

She'd been jealous of some strange woman called Sophia whom she'd never even met. She was still jealous of her, truth be told, because the queen wanted her and Simon to be a couple.

What on earth did the Queen of England's opinion have to do with her love life?

Did she even have a love life?

Her thoughts ran in all directions like rats fleeing a sinking ship, but her body didn't move at all. Simon's face grew closer until his lips touched hers. A flash of desire rose through her and her eyes shut tight as they kissed. Sparkles flashed across her brain and danced in her fingers and toes as chemistry rushed between them.

What was happening to her? She was the sensible one who drove her wilder friends home from parties. She didn't get into scrapes with their celebrity guests or have skeletons tucked behind the coats in her closets. Well, not until it turned out that she was the president's unknown love child. Everything seemed to have spiraled downhill since then.

Or was it uphill?

Simon's hands fisted in her blouse as their kiss deepened. Her fingers roamed into his thick, short-cropped hair. The rough skin of his cheek and his simple masculine scent thickened the arousal building inside her. His erection had thickened to the point where she could now feel it pressing against her belly. A pulse of thick, complicated desire throbbed and urged her to tighten their embrace.

Until a knock on the door made them fly apart.

Flushed and breathless, she smoothed her blouse as Simon strode to the door. He pulled it open a few inches and murmured that he preferred not to be disturbed. The invisible person on the other side mentioned something about an urgent phone call from Her Majesty.

Simon turned to her. "I'm afraid I must take this call. I'll be back in a moment."

The door closed and she was left alone in the strange sitting room. For the first time she noticed the painting above the fireplace, a clipper ship sailing across a stormy sea, tossing on the waves. An expensive-looking collection of porcelain lined the top of the mantel. What was she doing in this strange room—some kind of official den—groping a man who might one day be King of England. Had she lost her mind?

The queen must be calling to remind Simon of his royal duties and to urge him to keep his hands off strange American women.

Simon's absence did little to diminish her state of arousal. She wanted to hold him again. To kiss him. To rip his clothes off and make hot crazy love with him on the pale pink striped brocade of the sofa. She shoved a hand through her hair, only to discover that it was tangled from his fingers. She was madly smoothing it when the door opened again and Simon reappeared.

"Now, where were we?" Amusement glimmered in his eyes, along with desire.

A flame leapt inside her. She didn't remember ever feeling an attraction this strong. Her whole body seemed to gravitate toward him. Even while her brain issued warnings about how this liaison had no future and would likely end in disaster, her fingers snuck around his collar and into the hair at the nape of his neck, as their lips played together.

"What are we doing?" she managed, when they both came up for air. Her head spun from the intensity of the kisses.

"I'm not entirely sure but I know I like it." He nibbled her earlobe gently, which made her shiver with pleasure.

"Don't you think we should both be sensible?" She inhaled the scent of his skin and her fingers pressed into the muscle of his back.

"What's sensible?" His eyes were closed and his lips trailed over her face. Her skin hummed under his touch, under his breath, making her long to be closer to him than ever.

"I'm not sure I know anymore." She exhaled, longing to let go of her doubts and lose herself in Simon. He projected such confidence and self-assurance it was hard not to simply do what he said. He must have been a very effective army officer. "But my life is very wacky right now and I'm afraid of making it worse."

He laid a line of kisses along her neck, which had a frightening effect on her libido. "Am I making it worse?"

"Absolutely," she breathed. "Don't stop."

He chuckled, then kissed her full and firm on the mouth, embracing her with a caress that mingled power and strength with the utmost tenderness. So many emotions and sensations roamed through her that she almost wanted to cry.

When they finally stopped kissing and pulled apart, a deep sadness fell over her. The tiny separation foreshadowed the time when they'd say goodbye for the last time, because this relationship—if it even was a relationship—had no future. "If we have to keep this a secret, then it must be wrong." Her voice sounded thin and sad.

He opened his eyes and looked right at her. "Then let's not keep it a secret."

Five

Ariella paced around her apartment. Her phone had been ringing off the hook all morning. She couldn't ignore it because any call could easily be from an important client, but she was getting quite cagey about screening callers. The *Examiner* had printed a series of pictures of herself and Simon strolling through Georgetown the previous afternoon, so one more cat was out of the bag. She glanced at the familiar number with more than a little trepidation.

"Hi, Francesca."

"Ariella, you keep knocking it right out of the park."

"I know you're not talking about my softball swing."

"No, I'm talking about your ability to garner amazing publicity for the upcoming TV special. Liam says it will have the highest ratings of any show this year."

"Oh, yes. That." She went between regretting ever agreeing to it, and wanting to hurry up and get it over with. "Is there ever going to be a confirmed date for the taping?"

"They're still trying to get a firm commitment from the White House. That's about as easy as booking a date for the outbreak of a war. He's hoping for next week or the week after though. How about bringing your new royal boyfriend?"

"No way." She shoved a hand through her hair. "Besides, he has to go back to England for a bit." Her gut clenched. He'd phoned her only half an hour ago to say he'd be flying back that afternoon on urgent family business. How long would he be gone for? He did live there after all. Maybe he wouldn't come back and she'd be left to mop up one more scandal all by herself.

"You're a very dark horse."

"I totally am not. I'm the same person I've always been. It's the rest of the world that's crazy. Simon's a sweet man who happens to have been born into a famous family."

"Just like you happen to have been born to one."

She hesitated. "I guess you're right. He's not at all like you'd expect. Very unpretentious and genuine."

"And dead sexy."

"Yes. That, too." He seemed to grow more handsome every time she saw him. Or was that just because she was falling in love with him?

Her thoughts screeched to a halt. She was absolutely not allowed to fall in love with anyone on such short notice. Love was a big, long, lifetime thing that had to be carefully planned so that no one's heart got broken. She and Simon both agreed they didn't know where their... thing was going, and that they'd take it one step at a time.

"Didn't you realize the photographers would see you together?"

They had. In fact the photo opportunity was planned. They wanted to get it over with so they could stop meeting only in dark private corners surrounded by armed guards.

"Photographers see everything I do lately. They're always lurking about somewhere." It was a relief to shed the cloak of secrecy, but also alarming to give people one more thing to gossip about.

"Well, I'm so impressed with how you seem to take everything in stride. Anyone would think you'd been born in the public eye and handling it all your life."

"I suppose I'm like a duck where everything looks calm and smooth above the water, but underneath I'm paddling like mad." She needed to get to the gym so she could run off some energy on a machine. Otherwise she might explode.

"No way you're a duck, Ari. You're a swan. A royal swan."

She paced back into the kitchen and poured herself a cool glass of water. "There's nothing royal about me. I hope Simon's family aren't having a cow now that the story's broken in the press over there."

"How could they possibly not like you?"

Simon flew into Cardiff so he could drive directly to Dysart Castle in the Welsh Marches. The estate was the seat of his uncle Derek, the Duke of Aylesbury. It was Derek who had insisted in the strongest terms that he return to England and confront the "noxious" rumors about his affair with an American commoner.

Derek strode into the drawing room in his shooting jacket shortly before the usual lunch hour. He was damp from the mist of rain and had probably been out killing things since dawn. "Ah, you're here."

Master of the bleeding obvious, as usual. "You said it was urgent."

Derek peered at him from beneath his bushy salt-and-pepper brows. "Her Majesty is beside herself at the ugly stories splashed all over yesterday's papers. Your visit to the States has obviously grown overextended if the American press has the time and energy to invent silly stories about you."

"It's not a story. Ariella and I have grown close." And he looked forward to growing a lot closer. It had taken all his self-control to stop at kissing her. He'd managed because he knew there was something special about her, and he didn't want to do anything to endanger their budding relationship.

"Well, you'd better grow distant, immediately. You're second in line to the throne, man. You can't kiss any girl with a pretty smile who happens to cross your path."

Simon stiffened. "Ariella is not just anyone. She's intelligent, charming and has more poise than most of us royals put together."

"Don't be ridiculous. She's American. You remember what happened last time one of our family got involved with an American. He gave up the throne of England! Madness." Derek shrugged out of his jacket and tossed it over a gilded chair. "Break it off with her immediately and pray that she doesn't make a big fuss in the media."

"Ariella would never do such a thing. And I most certainly am not going to break it off with her."

Derek's already bilious face reddened further. "I thought your irresponsible and reckless days were behind you. Your older brother is married to a delightful and entirely suitable woman. Look upon him as an example."

"I honor and respect my brother and look forward to saluting him as my monarch. I feel confident that he will enjoy Ariella's company as much as I do."

"Don't be ridiculous. And she's the daughter of the president. We have enough trouble negotiating the maelstrom of American politics without you allying yourself with the daughter of one party's leader."

"She has never even met her father and politics plays no role in our relationship."

Derek had poured himself a stiff whiskey and swigged it. It was doubtless his third or fourth of the day despite the early hour. "Never even met her own father? Oh, yes. She's some kind of unwanted bastard who was given up for adoption. Perfect royal bride material."

Simon wanted to remind his uncle of the many "royal bastards" who had contributed to the country over the centuries, but he restrained himself. "Ariella and I are both adults, and quite capable of managing our affairs with dignity. I don't need any warnings or lessons or instructions in how to behave." Derek's miserable wife, Mary, was a pale shadow of the pretty, bright girl she'd once been. If there was any dire warning on how not to operate a relationship, Derek was it.

"Listen, Simon. If you get into some embarrassing international scrape it will be bad for all of us. Monarchies are in a battle for survival in the twenty-first century. An affair with this girl is tantamount to abandoning your duties. Next thing we know you'll be moving abroad."

Simon's hackles rose. "I'll never leave England. I know my duty to my country as well as to my own conscience."

His uncle's beady eyes narrowed. "The way you're acting you may well be asked to leave."

"You'd have to boot me out of the family first."

The older man sipped his whiskey and studied a painting of dead pheasants, bound by the neck into a lifeless bouquet. "Nothing is impossible."

The early morning air in England smelled fabulously exciting to Ariella. Even the fume-choked atmosphere

around the taxi rank at Heathrow Airport. She had a roster of back to back appointments stretching over the next
four days. Most of them had to do with the Duke of Buckingham's extravagant wedding. She had scheduled meetings with florists, caterers, makers of the finest crystal
and porcelain for the handcrafted tableware, the list was
almost endless.

But one appointment loomed in her mind above all
the others. At three-forty-five on Wednesday—two days
away—Ariella would finally meet the woman who gave
birth to her twenty-eight years ago. Her heart pounded
whenever she thought about it. How odd that this stranger
had carried her in her belly for nine long months.

And of course Simon was here. She'd told him of her
visit but warned him that she was very busy. She was here
to work and just because she'd kissed a prince did not mean
she could abandon her career and throw caution to the
wind. Her friends at home had warned her that the British
press were far more aggressive—and often crueler—than
the press at home, so she should watch her step. Still, hopefully they could manage a meeting. Her skin tingled every
time she thought about him. What would her mother think?

The question made her laugh aloud. The mom who
raised her, the sensible Montana housewife, would probably be full of dire warnings, issued in the most kind and
heartfelt way. She'd have much preferred to see Ariella
with the owner of a solid car dealership in Billings, or
perhaps a kindly bank manager in Bozeman.

But now she had another mother to think about. What
would Eleanor think about her relationship with Simon?
She was obviously concerned about her own privacy
and shrank from the spotlight, so she wasn't likely to be
thrilled.

Ariella's phone vibrated and she checked the number.

Think of the devil. "Hi, Simon." She couldn't help smiling as she said his name.

"You must be on British soil." His deep voice sent a flood of warmth to her belly.

"I am. Traveling over it in a taxi, to be precise."

"Where are you staying?"

"The Drake. It's a small hotel near Mayfair."

"Perfect. Right near St. James's Palace, my haunt when I'm in town. I'll pick you up at seven."

Temptation clawed at her. But her sense of duty won out. "I wish I could, but I'm meeting a potential client to pitch the most magnificent wedding in history. It will probably go quite late."

"I suppose asking you to come over after dinner isn't appropriate."

She smiled. "No, I suppose not."

"Lunch tomorrow at Buckingham Palace. Come meet the queen. She's never in town for long so it's a great opportunity for you two to get to know each other."

Ariella clutched the phone in a panic. "Oh, gosh, I have appointments all day tomorrow."

"That's a shame because she's heading to Scotland in the afternoon. But there'll be other times to meet her."

"I'm sorry I can't make it." Was it rude to say you'd rather spend the night in a meat locker than brave a lunch with one of the world's longest-reigning monarchs? Of course if things persisted with Simon, she'd eventually have to meet Her Majesty, but right now everything was very new and tentative and she had a feeling that no one would be rolling out the red carpet for her at the palace.

Not that she wanted them to. She didn't know what she wanted. "I'd love to see you, really I would, but…"

"Dinner tomorrow. My driver will pick you up with exquisite discretion. No one will know you're with me."

"I can't. I have a dinner meeting."

"That won't take all night."

She swallowed, and attempted a laugh. "I need to sleep, too. I wish I had more time for...fun, but this is a business trip." A pause made her nervous. Was he offended? It certainly wasn't good for business to snub a prince. She didn't want to book anything for after her mom's visit, as she was hoping they'd hit it off and spend hours together. "My last appointment is Thursday afternoon at three and my flight isn't until the next morning."

"So you can squeeze dinner with me into your busy schedule on Thursday?" Was he teasing or mad?

"I could, if that works for you. Of course if you're too busy, I quite understand." London whipped by outside her window, as rows of identical suburban houses gave way to more office buildings and shops.

"I'd clear my schedule in a heartbeat for the mere chance of laying eyes on you."

Okay, now he was kidding. "I don't think that will be necessary. Let's make plans closer to Thursday, okay? I hope nothing crazy happens between now and then, but you never know." She could hardly believe she was telling a prince that she couldn't commit to anything firm.

"I'm penciling it in." She could hear the irony in his voice. "And call me at once if there's anything you need. Our entire nation is at your disposal."

"Thanks." She grinned. "Much appreciated."

She shook her head as she put her phone away. How had her life changed so much in six short months? There were even photographers at the airport, though she doubted they'd get much money for photos of her in jeans and with her hair in a messy bun, carrying her luggage to the taxi rank. There was so much to be excited about, sometimes it was hard to remember that she had plenty to be afraid of as well.

Meeting her reclusive mother, hopefully meeting her famous father and now a romance with a man who made her smile each time she thought of him. It was all just a little too fabulous. Rather like teetering on a tightrope between two skyscrapers. She had to keep her chin up, her eyes forward and put one foot in front of the other, and hopefully in another six months she'd be in an even better place, where everything wasn't quite so strange and precarious.

"You come from America?" The cab driver's loud Cockney voice jolted her from her thoughts. He didn't wait for an answer. "You 'eard about this girl who's supposed to be the daughter of your president?"

She froze. Did he recognize her? He looked in his side mirror and changed lanes. "I'm not sure who you mean."

"Pretty girl. Long brown 'air. Looks a bit like you." His eyes fixed on hers again in the mirror. She blinked. "Papers say she's 'avin' an affair with our Prince Simon. Some people have all the luck, don't they?"

"Oh, yes." She pretended to text on her phone, keeping her head down. Maybe he was fishing for information he could sell to the London tabloid that always had a bare-breasted woman on page three. "Very lucky."

She kept her head down until they pulled up in front of her hotel. Mercifully there wasn't a photographer in sight and she checked in and changed, telling herself to be prepared for anything.

Frustration made Simon spring from his chair and pace across the room. How could Ariella be right here in his own country and too busy to see him? Their few days of separation had him in an agony of anticipation. Now he had to wait until Thursday to see her?

He called her on Monday night, hoping that her dinner meeting would be over and they could plan a moonlit tryst. No dice. She was still in consultation with a client, and she wouldn't even reveal the person's name. He rather suspected it was his schoolmate Toby Buckingham, and he tried calling him to intercept from another direction, but Toby didn't even answer.

On Tuesday morning he tried again, hoping for a quick tea, only to be politely brushed off. Restless as hell by Wednesday afternoon, he threw on a panama hat that covered his face and decided to stroll the short distance from St James's Palace to Buckingham Palace. Maybe he'd go for a ride on one of the queen's horses. He told his driver, who doubled as security, to head there without him so he could get some fresh air. David didn't make a fuss. He knew that nothing was likely to happen on the quiet streets between the two palaces, and Simon had his phone if needed.

He was walking briskly, trying to banish the vision of Ariella's intoxicating beauty from his mind, when a girl walking along the other side of the street, in the opposite direction, caught his eye.

She walked exactly like Ariella. Long-legged, and graceful as a gazelle, with the slightly loping stride of someone in a hurry. But this woman had shoulder-length blond hair. Large dark glasses hid her face. He turned and stared after her as she passed.

That was Ariella's walk. And those were her shoes. The sight of those simple black ballet flats she favored sent a jolt of adrenaline to his own feet. He turned, following her, still on the opposite side of the street.

Why would she be in disguise? The hair must be a wig. The neat black skirt did nothing to disguise the elegant swing of her hips. He'd recognize that walk anywhere.

Who was she hiding from? She had no reason to conceal her movements to plan the big wedding she was here to organize. She was used to photographers tracking her and mostly ignored them, as he'd witnessed on several occasions in D.C.

She was doing something that she didn't want anyone to know about. Including him.

She crossed the road to his side and he slowed his pace and hung back a little. Not that she even glanced at him. She was lost in a world of her own, barely noticing the other people on the pavement. She walked fast, but he had no trouble keeping up.

Why are you following her?

Because I want to know where she's going.

Something in his gut told him that this was wrong. She had a right to privacy. In fact they'd had several long discussions about how much they valued their right to privacy, which was often under siege. Somehow, that didn't stop him.

She turned left, down a small side road. She hesitated and pulled a phone out of her pocket, causing him to stop in his tracks. A man walking behind him bumped into him, and by the time he'd apologized she was walking again. Talking on the phone.

He couldn't hear what she was saying, but her singsong laugh was unmistakable. Which confirmed what he already knew. Ariella Winthrop was walking through Mayfair in disguise, and he was going to find out why.

Why hadn't she told him where she was going? Fresh from defending her to his suspicious family, he found doubts sneaking into his mind. He knew she wouldn't leak stories of their romance to the media. Would she? Not that there was anything to leak, though he intended to change that as soon as humanly possible.

Could it be something to do with her famous father? They hadn't spoken much about him. She seemed to find the subject awkward, considering that she'd never met him.

Or was there another man in her life? His mind and body recoiled from the idea and he didn't believe it for a moment. But where was she going?

She turned left and he hurried to keep up, in case she disappeared into one of the tall Edwardian buildings lining the street. She'd tucked her phone back into her purse and strode on, looking intently ahead. Then she stopped.

This time he glanced behind him before halting, to avoid a collision. She pulled out a piece of paper and glanced up at the plaque on the house. Then she climbed the steps, rang a bell, and entered through a pair of heavy wood doors.

He approached the building a full minute later and paused as discreetly as possible in front of the doorway. The Westchester Club. He had no idea what that was, only that he wanted to gain entry. He strolled to the end of the block, pretended to casually consult a No Parking sign and considered his options.

Ariella's heart pounded as she climbed into the elevator and pressed a button. It was the old-fashioned kind of elevator with the sliding iron gates, and hearing the porter slam them behind her didn't help her nerves. Her mother was waiting for her on the fifth floor.

Scarlet had suggested this private club as a venue. Rooms were available for rent only to the most exclusive groups, and Scarlet had called in a favor to secure one for this afternoon, since it was near Ariella's hotel so she could get there without attracting attention.

She pulled off the cheesy blond wig she'd bought to keep photographers off her scent, and loosed her hair from its bun. The elevator jerked to a halt on the fifth floor. She hauled back the iron gate and stepped out onto a polished wood floor. The hallway contained three tall doors, and she was wondering which one was number 503, when one of the doors opened.

"Ariella?" The tentative voice came from a slender, pretty woman with curly light brown hair.

"Yes?" There was a question in her voice, as if she wasn't quite sure who she was any more. She wanted to greet the woman as "Mom," but that seemed presumptuous. Her heart beat so fast she could hardly speak. "You must be Eleanor."

Eleanor's hands had risen to cover her mouth as tears welled in her big green eyes. Eyes almost exactly like her own. "You're so beautiful. Even more so than in the photos."

"You're sweet. And you look far too young to be the mother of a twenty-eight-year-old." She looked like she was still in her thirties, with smooth pale skin and a girlish figure.

"I am too young to be the mother of a twenty-eight-year-old." She shrugged and smiled. "That was the problem, really. I got pregnant when I was too young to be ready." Tears ran down her cheeks. "And I missed out on so much."

Eleanor seemed ready to lose it, and Ariella wanted to comfort her, but didn't know how. She ushered her back into the room, which was a large drawing room with several graciously upholstered sofas. "Shall we sit down?"

"Oh, yes." Eleanor pulled out a tissue and wiped her face. "I'm sorry I'm making such a fool of myself. It's just that…I've waited so long for this moment and I wasn't sure it would ever come."

"Me, too. I can hardly believe we're finally getting to meet." They sat next to each other on the plush sofa, and she took Eleanor's hands in her own and squeezed them. Her skin was cool and soft. Cold hands, warm heart. The cliché popped into her mind. "Thank you so much for coming to London to see me."

"It's my great pleasure. I'm too afraid to travel to the States. I feel like they'd know who I was when I go through airport security and there'd be a big to do." Eleanor had picked up an Irish lilt to her voice. "I'm very shy, really. That's one of the reasons why I knew I wouldn't be good for Ted. He was always so outgoing and friendly and loved to be around people."

Ariella realized that Ted was the man she still thought of as the president of the United States. "Was he your boyfriend?" She only knew what she'd read in the papers, and she knew from firsthand experience they weren't always a reliable source.

Eleanor sighed. "He was. We dated our junior and senior years in high school. I was so in love!" Her soft eyes looked distant. "Even then he had big plans and intended to go away to college. He dreamed of being a Rhodes Scholar and studying abroad, and then he wanted to join the Peace Corps and travel. He always had such grand ambitions."

"Well, he's achieved the highest office an American can attain."

Eleanor nodded. Her mouth tightened for a moment, her lip almost quivering. Ariella ached to put her arms around this delicate and nervous woman, but didn't want to frighten her. "I never did really understand what he saw in me. He said he found me very peaceful." Her eyes twinkled with the memory.

"I'm sure an energetic and outgoing man needs peace more than anyone."

She smiled at Ariella. "Maybe so. My husband, Greg, was a quiet man. Not as exciting as Ted but a good man who I shared a happy marriage with for twenty-three years. He died of a heart attack. Far too young, he was." Tears welled in her eyes again.

"I'm sorry. I would have liked to meet him."

Eleanor's gaze focused on her. "Did you tell me that you've never met Ted?"

Ariella swallowed and shook her head. "Not yet, but…" She paused. It sounded pathetic really. Embarrassing. How could they have gone all this time—nearly two months since the DNA test results were released—without any contact at all?

"I'm sure Ted wants to meet you. I know it in my heart." She squeezed Ariella's hands. "They must be keeping him from you. You must reach out to him."

"I've been talking to ANS about doing a taped reunion. It should take place soon."

"On television?" Eleanor's eyes widened into shock.

She nodded. "My friend Francesca's husband is president of the network. Apparently the White House is almost ready to agree to a date."

Eleanor winced. "A private meeting would be so much nicer."

"I know, but the president isn't a private person, really. Not to the point where I could call him up and introduce myself. Somehow it seemed more…doable."

"You're outgoing, too, aren't you?" She smiled slightly.

"I suppose I am. I plan parties for a living. I love getting people together and making it an occasion to remember."

She smiled again. "You must get that from Ted. You have his cheekbones, too. And that sparkle of determination he always had in his eye."

"I think you and I look alike, too." She drank in the precious sight of her birth mother's face. "Our faces are similar shapes, and we're both tall and slim."

"Will o' the Wisp, Ted used to call me. Said a strong breeze would blow me away one day. I suppose in a way he was right. It blew me over to Ireland and I didn't dare to look back."

"I'm sure he'd love to see you again."

Her eyes widened into a look of panic. "Oh, no. No. I'm sure he'd never forgive me for what I did. I thought it was for the best but looking back I can see that not telling him he had a child was a terrible thing to do. An act of cowardice. I won't forgive myself and I wouldn't expect him to, either."

Not knowing her famous father, Ariella wasn't really in a position to argue with her. "Why didn't you tell him?"

"I knew he'd do *the right thing.*" She said it with mocking emphasis. "Not the right thing for him and the big career he'd dreamed of, but the right thing in the eyes of our parents and pastors and neighbors. He'd settle down in our small town in Montana and live a tiny fraction of the live he'd imagined, because he'd be forced to support a family instead of going off to the big college he'd won a scholarship to. I could never let him throw away his future like that."

"You could have let him make the decision himself."

"I know. Now I know that." Tears welled in her eyes again. "I didn't want him to grow to hate me so I did the one thing that should truly make him hate me. I gave away our child and never told him she existed." She broke down into sobs.

Unable to hold back any longer, Ariella wrapped her arms around Eleanor's slim shoulders and held her tight, her own tears falling. "Everything happens for a reason," she said softly. "Maybe we'll never even know the true reason, but I believe that all the same."

"You're a very clever girl. I can see that in your eyes."

Eleanor dabbed at her own eyes with a tissue. "You have your dad's keen intelligence. I bet you have a university degree, don't you?"

Ariella nodded. "In history, from Georgetown."

"It's such a coincidence that both you and Ted wound up living in Washington, D.C." She blew her nose.

"It is strange."

At that moment the door opened and their heads swung around. Ariella gasped when she saw Simon standing in the doorway.

Six

"Ariella." Simon had a hat clutched in his hand and a curiously intense expression on his face.

Eleanor gasped and brought her wet tissue to her face as if she wanted to hide behind it.

"What are you doing here?" Ariella's voice came out sounding stern.

"I…" He hesitated. A sheepish expression crossed his handsome features. "I confess that I saw you on the street and followed you."

"What?" Anger surged inside her, warring with the sharp sting of attraction. "What made you think you could follow me into a private meeting?"

He shrugged. "I'm embarrassed to say that I didn't examine my motives too closely." He looked at Eleanor, as if expecting an introduction.

"You need to leave." Ariella rose to her feet. She could feel Eleanor, desperate to preserve her privacy, shrinking back into the shell that she'd started to emerge from. "You may be a prince but that doesn't mean you can march in anywhere you feel like."

"You're absolutely right, of course. My sincerest apologies." He nodded and bowed to Eleanor, and started to back out the door.

"Wait!" She couldn't just let him go. Damn it. Angry as she was, she wanted to see him too badly. She turned to Eleanor. "This is my...boyfriend." She dared Simon to argue with her word choice. "Is it okay if I introduce you?"

Eleanor gulped, but nodded shyly.

"Simon Worth, this is Eleanor Daly. My mother." Her throat swelled with emotion as she said the word *mother*.

Eleanor stared. "*Prince* Simon Worth?"

Simon bowed. "At your service. It's an honor to meet you, Mrs. Daly." He swept forward, took her hand and shook it warmly, while she gazed at him in shock. "I know Ariella's been looking forward to this for a long time."

"Goodness." She stared from one of them to the other, as if she wasn't sure what was going to happen next.

A feeling shared by her daughter. "Simon encouraged me to meet you. I wasn't sure you'd want to."

"I'm so glad the two of you are finally getting together." Simon glowed with confidence and good cheer, as usual. "It seems a wonderful thing to come out of the wiretapping scandal."

Eleanor still looked shell-shocked. "I saw a headline about the two of you at the newsagent and I just assumed it was more made-up rubbish."

"Sometimes there's a grain of truth in the wild stories the press invent." Simon smiled. "I'm happy to confirm that this is one of them."

"So you two are actually...dating?" Eleanor stared from Simon to Ariella.

"We're not quite sure what we're doing." Ariella jumped in, not wanting Simon to be put on the spot. She couldn't even imagine how the royal family might be reacting to news of their romance. Simon hadn't mentioned the topic, which wasn't too encouraging. "We enjoy each other's company."

"Oh." Eleanor's brow furrowed with concern. Ariella got the sense that she'd love to issue some stern warnings, but was too polite. She probably wasn't happy that her newfound daughter was embarking on a relationship that wasn't likely to end in a glorious happy-ever-after.

Because really, did she expect Simon to marry her?

The whole idea was ridiculously premature. They hadn't even done more than kiss yet. She glanced at Simon, whose eyes met hers and sent a zap of heat straight to her core. It would have been so much easier if she could have avoided him. This week was hectic enough already.

"I'll leave the two of you in peace." Simon must have read her thoughts. He nodded nobly to Eleanor, and squeezed Ariella's hand, then turned and disappeared out the door. Ariella couldn't manage to think of anything polite to say, so they both stared after him in silence until the door closed behind him.

"Goodness." Eleanor looked dazed.

"Life has been pretty intense this year." They both sat back down on the sofa. "Sometimes I wonder what else could possibly happen."

"Don't tempt fate." Her mother patted her hand. "But I do hope you get to meet your father soon. I'm so proud of him for being elected president, and I know he's going to do a wonderful job running the country. He's off to a great start already. Almost makes me think I should move back."

Adrenaline surged through Ariella. "You should. It would be so wonderful to have you near. Come live in

D.C.! Georgetown, where I live, is quite peaceful really. Lots of trees and lovely old buildings."

"You make it sound very inviting. Perhaps I have been living in the back of beyond for too long. Hiding away, I suppose."

"You don't have to hide from anyone now."

Eleanor looked doubtful. "I don't think I could face all those reporters the way you and Ted have. I'd be tongue-tied and embarrass both of you."

"You couldn't possibly embarrass either of us. I bet it would be a huge relief to come forward and get it over with. Why don't you come back to the States with me at the end of the week? I'm leaving on Friday and I can probably get you a ticket on the same plane if I call in a favor or two."

Eleanor's hand stiffened. "I…I'm not ready for that." Once again she felt her mother shrinking away from her. "But I'd very much like to stay in touch with you by phone, and maybe I'll gradually pluck up the courage to at least come visit you there. And maybe take a trip up to Montana to see all the old friends I've avoided for so long. I never told a single soul there about my pregnancy and I'm sure they all wondered what happened when I just disappeared. I stayed in a special home for unwed mothers way outside of town until I was due, and then I took all my saved pennies and left for Chicago after the birth. I couldn't face any of them knowing I'd given away my own child. Ted's child. I met Greg there. He'd come from Ireland for the summer to work as a roofer and he swept me off my feet." Her sad eyes sparkled a little when she spoke about him. "With him I started a new chapter of my life. I never looked back. I felt that if I did I'd fall off some cliff and get swallowed by all the emotion I tried so hard not to feel during that time." Her pale eyes grew glassy with tears again.

"It's not good to avoid your true feelings. Sooner or later they'll come back to bite you. I learned that after my adoptive parents were killed. All that pain is scary, but once you come to terms with it you can move forward. Until then you're stuck in a place of fear." She squeezed her mother's hands, which had softened again.

"You're very wise, Ariella."

"I wish I was. I just try to handle one crisis at a time. In my job there's always another one coming so there's no point in getting ahead of yourself."

They laughed, and, taking a cue from the sudden intimacy, Ariella hugged her birth mother for the very first time.

Simon refused to let Ariella leave England without visiting his home. He promised that he wouldn't stalk her around London or corner her in private drawing rooms as long as she'd agree to postpone her return flight until the following Monday so she could spend the weekend with him at Whist Castle. He insisted that, in her line of work, staying at one of England's great country houses counted as research and client cultivation. After a little persuasion, and a conversation with her business partner, Scarlet, she agreed.

He had the staff prepare his mother's favorite bedroom for Ariella, ostensibly because it had such beautiful views over the lake, but mostly because it had a door connecting it with his own bedroom. It had taken all his gentlemanly self-control to keep all their activities above the neck so far, and he intended to steer them both into unexplored territory this weekend.

His driver brought Ariella up from London on Thursday evening. He had a full schedule of activities planned to keep her entertained and give her a slice of English country life, and he intended to introduce her to the family at a charity polo match taking place nearby on Sunday. This weekend would be an excellent taste of the pleasures and realities of life in the royal family.

The realities, of course, might scare her. There was no denying that his family had rather fixed ideas about whom he should marry. Someone British, with aristocratic heritage and a featureless past that could not draw comment in the press. Of course he'd informed them that he would marry for no reason other than love, but he wasn't entirely sure they'd listened. He'd been raised to believe that duty trumped all other considerations, including happiness. So far he'd managed to find his own happiness within the confines of his duty, creating opportunities where he saw them. There was no denying that choosing Ariella as his bride would likely draw censure and disapproval.

On the other hand there was no good reason for them to oppose her, and sooner or later they usually saw reason. He just hoped they wouldn't frighten her too badly.

He tested the handle on the connecting bedroom door, and pocketed the key. No sense filling his head with plans then finding himself locked out. His body throbbed with anticipation of being alone with Ariella. From the first moment he'd seen her, across the ballroom at that gala event, he'd had a powerful sense that she was the one. So far he'd managed to battle all the forces standing between them, and now he was within reach of holding her—naked— in his arms. The prospect heated his blood and fired his imagination.

He hovered at the front windows looking for the approaching car, fighting the urge to phone and see how far away she was, then practically ran down the stairs when it finally nosed up the drive. He couldn't remember being this eager to see anyone, ever.

Ariella looked radiant, as usual, in a simple black dress, with her long hair flowing over her shoulders. A smile spread across her pretty face as she saw him, and he felt his own face reflect it back. "Welcome to Whist Castle."

"It's every bit as beautiful as I'd imagined."

"I'm glad you think so, too, and you haven't even seen the grounds yet. Come in." He fought the urge to slip his arm around her waist, which took a great deal of self-control. "How did your meeting with your mother go?"

"It was amazing." He glanced at her and saw her smile. "I'd been so worried that she'd seem like a stranger, that maybe we wouldn't even recognize each other. But I felt an instant connection with her."

"That's fantastic. Do you think you'll see her again soon?"

She hesitated. "I don't know. I really hope so. She's still deathly afraid of publicity and the criticism she'll face for giving me up and not telling Ted Morrow about me. I got all carried away and started trying to convince her to move to D.C."

He laughed. "That sounds like the kind of thing I'd do."

"Too much, too soon?" She smiled. "And then I tried to talk her into visiting Montana with me. I hope I didn't scare her right away."

"I'm sure she's privately thrilled that you're so glad to meet her and that you want to spend more time with her."

"I hope so. I really liked her. I plan to call her regularly, and hopefully we'll build the relationship and take it from there."

Words to live by. He counseled himself to take the same course with Ariella. Just because he felt a deep conviction that they were meant to be together did not mean that she felt the same way. Gentle persuasion and thoughtfully paced seduction would be the sensible path for him to take, no matter how loudly his more primitive urges begged him to take her in his arms and kiss her hard on the mouth.

He showed her to her room, glancing at the door to his own, but not mentioning it. There would be time for that later. Then he took her on a brief tour of his favorite place in the world—the great hall that had once been a Saxon throne room, and had hosted many riotous dinner parties during his reign there. Then they walked to the oldest part of the building, which held the gallery of paintings collected over the centuries by his ancestors, which included works by Raphael, Titian, Rembrandt, Caravaggio and El Greco, among others.

Ariella was suitably poleaxed. "I think you have a better collection than most museums."

"I know. I do lend them out to museums from time to time so they're not entirely hidden away in my lair. I am lucky to have had ancestors with such good taste."

"Have you ever had your portrait painted?" She glanced up at a majestic Van Dyke portrait of a young Charles II.

"Never. They'd have to nail me down to keep me still enough."

"I think that's a shame. I'd love to be able to stare at a magnificent painting of you."

"Why, when you can eyeball the real thing?" They'd been unabashedly eyeing each other since she walked through the door. Their days apart had created sexual tension thick enough to fog windows.

"What kind of setting do you think would suit you?" She looked him up and down, as if wondering whether a landscape or interior might be better. His skin heated under his clothes as her green gaze drifted from his face, to his torso, and lower…

"Definitely the outdoors. Hanging off a mountain, maybe."

"That's a great idea. And these days they can snap a picture to work from so you only have to stay in the same place for a microsecond. Think of all those poor starving artists who would love to become the royal court painter. I think it's your duty to be a patron of the arts."

"I hadn't looked at it that way."

She swept down the hallway, and he hesitated for a moment to enjoy the swinging motion of her hips inside her fitted dress, before striding after her.

Simon's castle was very ancient, but with wear from centuries of loving use, it felt like a home rather than a monument. And Simon thought of everything to make her comfortable: tea and scones on the terrace overlooking a lake with water lilies in full bloom, an art collection that could make you weep with its magnificence and a sunlit bedroom with a view of the lake.

Still, she wasn't entirely relaxed. This weekend would undoubtedly take their relationship to a new level, one way or another. She was on his turf, at his mercy. She had no idea what he had planned for the weekend and he'd told her not to worry, she was in good hands. Which made her very nervous. She was used to being in charge and making plans and booking the entertainment. What if he decided to spring the queen on her as a surprise? With Simon around she knew she'd better be prepared for anything.

"I told the staff we'll fend for ourselves at dinner." Simon led her back from the art gallery into a sweeping living room with a high wooden ceiling. "I make a mean spag bol."

"Is that a British way of saying spaghetti bolognese?"

He winked. "And they say Americans don't bother to learn other languages."

He was actually going to cook? She'd tell her beating heart to be still if she thought it would do any good. Dressed in khakis and a white shirt, he looked classically handsome. And the ever present twinkle of mischief in his eyes always sent her pulse racing. "I'll have you know I speak Spanish and French, and I intend to study Chinese as soon as I can find the time."

He smiled. "I'm impressed. Of course I'd have expected no less of you. You're disturbingly perfect."

"I am not." She felt her face heat. Now he was making her blush? So much for her famous cool and poised demeanor. "I have many flaws."

"Name one. No, wait." He walked across the room to a wooden cabinet, then pulled out a bottle of wine. "I think we'll enjoy an excellent wine while we discuss your flaws." He uncorked the bottle with muscular ease, and poured the rich red wine into two glasses.

Her flaws? Was this like a job interview where she was supposed to have flaws like being too much of a perfectionist, or excessively punctual? Or could she be honest?

It's not like she was trying to get him to fall in love with her.

Their fingers touched as she took the glass from him, sending a jolt of warmth to her core. "One flaw. Hmm. I'm a terrible speller. I always have to get someone to re-read important documents. I'm quite capable of spelling my own name wrong."

"That's nothing. I'm dyslexic."

"Are you really? I had no idea."

"So you'll need a more impressive flaw than that, I'm afraid." They settled into a wide leather sofa. He peered at her as he sipped his wine. "A fatal flaw, perhaps. Or else I'll just keep insisting that you're perfect."

"I can be quite impatient."

"Nonsense. Look at how you've handled the press. Most

women would have had a tantrum or two by now. Next!"
His eyes sparkled.

"Hmm…" What could she say to shock him out of his
amused complacency? "I'm a reformed nymphomaniac."

His eyebrows rose slightly, but the rest of his expression
didn't change. "Not too reformed, I hope."

"You're terrible." She couldn't help laughing. "The truth
is I'm probably the opposite. Too uptight. Maybe that's
my flaw."

"That can be fixed." Heat flickered between them as
their eyes met in silence. A couple of buttons were open
at the neck of his shirt, revealing a tantalizing sliver of
rather tanned chest. His neck was thick and muscular, like
an athlete's, and she was pretty confident that the rest of
him would be, too.

He shifted closer to her on the sofa. Their thighs touched
and she wondered what he'd look like naked. Then she
wondered if she was going to find out tonight. Anxiety
crept through her, along with the steady pulse of desire.
Having sex with a prince wasn't something you could easily forget. Yet that's what she'd have to do, eventually, as
she was hardly going to become a member of the royal
family.

"Your brain is going a million miles an hour." His face
drew close to hers.

"There's another flaw. I think too much."

"No one's ever accused me of that. I'm known for acting first and thinking later." He grinned. She could smell
his intoxicating musky scent. "It's gotten me into some
scrapes over the years."

"And I have a feeling it's about to get you into another
one unless we put our wine down." Their lips were moving inexorably closer.

"You do think of everything." He took her glass and placed it on the floor next to his. "Now, where were we?"

She didn't have time to think of an answer, as his mouth closed over hers and his big arms wrapped around her. A sigh escaped her as she fell into his embrace. The days apart had been torture. Trying to stop herself from thinking about him, from wanting to see him. Then behaving appropriately in front of the drivers and the butler and all those other people constantly hovering around.

Now it was just her and Simon. Their kiss deepened and his tongue flicked against hers. The throb low in her belly grew more urgent, her nipples straining against the cups of her bra. But surely there was security or someone nearby? "Should we go somewhere more private?" she whispered. At night she was haunted by visions of photographers peeking in her windows, trailing her to the most mundane places and pouncing on her.

He didn't answer, but swept their glasses up and nodded for her to follow. They strode through the silent house. It wasn't dark outside. It stayed light until late in England in the summer, so it felt oddly like midafternoon though it must be at least eight. Why was she thinking about the time?

Because at this very moment she was about to climb into bed with a prince. At least she assumed it would be a bed. Knowing Simon she could well be wrong.

She followed him upstairs, and she felt a flush of relief when he turned into his own bedroom.

Condoms! Was now the right moment to mention the need for contraception? Or was that presumptuous? She took one look at the large bed. "Um, I have some condoms in my luggage."

He turned around with a smile. "Hmm. Maybe you

weren't lying about being a slightly reformed nympho-maniac."

"Or is it just that I'm annoyingly prepared for everything?"

"I suspect the latter. And don't worry, I have some specially purchased for the occasion."

"How does a prince buy condoms? I mean, you can't wander into Boots the Chemist on your local high street and slam them down on the counter with a smile."

"Why not?" He pulled a packet of Trojans from an elegant mahogany chest.

"Um, because everyone would know what you're up to."

"And they'd be jealous." He stepped toward her and stole her breath with a hot, urgent kiss. "But don't worry. My secretary purchases them in a cunningly anonymous fashion."

His fingers worked their way around the zipper on the side of her dress. Then he seemed stymied. Her breasts tingled at the thought of him touching them. "I have to lift it over my head," she rasped.

"No." He looked thoughtfully at the garment. "*I* have to lift it over your head." He lifted the hem and she held her breath and raised her arms as he pulled the dress up and off. With her dress crumpled like a tissue in his broad hands, he surveyed her—wordless—for a moment. She should feel self-conscious standing there in her bra and panties, but she didn't. Simon's desire was every bit as naked as her body.

She kicked off her shoes and tackled the buttons on his shirt, while he undid his belt and stepped out of his pants. Good grief. His chest was thick muscle, highlighted by a line of sun-bleached golden hair that pointed to the fierce erection seeking freedom from his conservative boxer shorts.

"Let me help you with that," she murmured, tugging the cotton down over his thighs. She realized too late that she was licking her lips. It had been a long time since she'd had sex and her entire body sizzled with anticipation. His legs were sturdy as the oak trees on his estate, with knees scarred by countless adventures, and she enjoyed the movement of his muscles as he stepped out of his underwear.

He unsnapped her bra before she had even stood up again, and her breasts pointed at him in accusation of arousing her past the point of decency.

At long last.

Together they pulled off her panties, then their bodies met, his erection fitting neatly against her belly. They breathed heavily, skin heating as they managed a very tentative kiss: a wisp of tongue, a graze of teeth, the tiniest, smooth, teasing and taunting until they couldn't stand it anymore. Then they fell onto the bed and Simon crawled over her, covering her with his body, with his kisses, tasting and testing her skin until she moaned with urgency.

He rolled on the condom and entered her carefully. Their eyes met for a moment, and the look of concern on his handsome face made her smile. She lifted her hips to welcome him and enjoyed his expression of rapture as his eyes slid closed and he sank deep inside her.

Pleasure coursed through her at the feel of his big, strong body wrapped around hers. She moved with him easily, enjoying sudden and intense relief from all the tension that had built between them in the short time they'd known each other.

"Ariella." He rasped her name with a hint of surprise, as if discovering it for the first time. Somehow it jerked her back to the reality of who she was. Ariella Winthrop, whose life had been turned upside down by the scandalous

circumstances of her birth and now by a shocking international romance. Even as she writhed in Simon's arms she
couldn't help wondering if this was all a crazy mistake.
Would she wake up soaked in regret at compounding the
madness that was her life lately?

If the press found out she and Simon had slept together
they'd have a field day. They'd be clamoring for snapshots
of the "royal smooch" or any casual indiscretion.

She'd let this whole thing spiral out of control. In D.C.,
she could have easily kept Simon at arm's length until
he went back to Britain, instead of embarking on an ill-
advised romance that would have people whispering and
gossiping behind her back.

"Ariella." He said it again.

"Yes?" Was he asking a question?

"I just like saying it. Celebrating it. That we're here together at last."

She chuckled, then carefully maneuvered them until she
was on top. "You're a hard man to resist." That was the
truth. You couldn't say no to Simon. At least she couldn't.

She leaned forward to kiss him, then her hair trailed
over his chest as she rose and moved over him. His eyes
closed and his face wore an expression of sheer bliss as
she rode him. His hands wandered over her chest, enjoying the curve of her breasts and circling her waist. Then
he deftly changed positions again and took back the lead.

Thoughts slipped away as he drove her deep into a world
where worries didn't exist. Nothing mattered but their two
bodies, moving in sync, holding and clutching at each
other, their breath mingling and their skin sticking together
as they edged closer and closer to the inevitable climax.

Afterward they lay in each other's arms, as countless
other couples must have done over the years in this same

grand chamber. Dukes, princes and earls, wives, mistresses and probably a few comely servant girls as well.

"What are we doing?" She breathed into his ear. It wasn't the first time she'd voiced the thought aloud.

"We're in the throes of a passionate romance," he answered.

"You make things seem so simple."

"Usually they are simple, and people go out of their way to make them complicated."

"But how long can it go on for? You live here and I live in D.C. It's silly."

"It's wonderful." He stroked her hair, his eyes soft.

She exhaled slowly. "It is."

"So we need to enjoy our passionate romance one day at a time and see where it takes us."

"With the press breathing down our necks?"

He shrugged. "They'll do what they want to do, regardless of what we want or hope for. I try to ignore them in general. Unless I need some PR for World Connect. Then I'm all smiles and pithy sound bites." He grinned.

"I need to cultivate that attitude." She rested her head on his broad chest. "They're just doing their job. As you said before, they're not likely to leave me alone any time soon because of the president being my father, so I might as well get used to them."

"Good, because on Sunday we're going to a charity polo match and there will be plenty of press there." He had that mischievous look again.

"Uh-oh."

"It'll be fun. And you'll get to meet my family."

Anxiety spiked through her. "Your older brother and his wife?"

"They're away on a tour of Australia, but you'll meet

my grandmother and assorted cousins, aunts and uncles. And my younger brother will be there."

She swallowed, trying not to let her panic show. "Your grandmother...the queen?"

"Don't be intimidated. She looks fierce from a distance but up close she's very warm and easy to talk to."

She blew out a breath. "I hope I won't stutter like an idiot."

"You are the last person on earth to feel flummoxed in the presence of royalty. Especially since you're already sleeping with it."

She chuckled. "There is that." Then her gut churned. "Does the queen know? I mean, about us?"

"If she reads the papers she will." He stroked her cheek. "Don't worry. My family will love you. It will be fun."

Fun. Ariella very much doubted that it would be fun. Intimidating, alarming, fraught with potential pitfalls? Yes. Fun? Not so much.

Either way, in less than two days, she'd find out.

Seven

Ariella tried everything she could think of to get out of attending the polo match. The Duke of Buckingham had officially hired them for the wedding so she really should be in London scouting out suppliers for the party. But, yes, it would be a Sunday and in England most things were closed on Sunday. She should get back to the U.S. and… well, yes, it would still be Sunday.

So on Sunday morning she found herself combing her hair with shaking hands.

Simon opened the door dividing their rooms and looked in. He smiled when he saw her. "Just checking that you haven't climbed out the window."

"What if they all hate me?"

"They'll love you." His ebullient confidence did nothing to soothe her frazzled nerves.

"I don't know anything about polo."

"You don't need to. Clap when our team scores and you'll be good."

"What if a reporter asks probing questions?"

"They won't. It's a very exclusive event and there are unwritten rules that keep them at a respectful distance."

"What if I become hysterical and make a big scene?"

He grinned. "Then we'll call some nice men in white coats to come take you away. Would you like a glass of Pimm's to soothe your nerves?"

"No, thanks. I really don't like to drink before noon. Especially on Sunday. It affects my aim." She brandished her mascara wand.

"Quite understandable. I should probably warn you about my uncle Derek. He's likely to be three sheets to the wind by noon and isn't shy about expressing himself."

Uncle Derek? She'd never heard of him. Her confusion must have shown in her face.

"He's my mother's brother, so not royal by birth, but he's latched on to the family and is hanging on with a death grip. He tries to be more traditional than anyone so he's not likely to approve of me dating an American."

She sighed. "It's not like we're…serious." Was she trying to convince herself? Their weekend together had been so easy and fun. She and Simon really clicked. They could talk about anything. And the sex…

"Says who?" He sauntered into the room. "I can be very serious when the occasion calls for it." He walked up behind her where she stood at the mirror and slid his arms around her waist. His lips pressed hotly into her neck and sent heat plunging to her toes. "And I seriously like you."

She blinked, looking from her startled face to his relaxed one in the mirror. "I like you, too, but it is a strange situation, you have to admit."

"My entire life is a strange situation, by most measurable parameters." He nibbled on her ear, which made her gasp. "I don't let it bother me."

"I guess when you put it that way…" Her words trailed off as their eyes locked in the mirror. His managed to sparkle with amusement and desire at the same time. His hands roamed over her hips and belly, setting off tremors of desire. Last night's lovemaking still reverberated in her mind and body. If she could just get through this afternoon without any drama they'd be back in bed together, tonight. Their last night before her flight back to D.C. tomorrow.

Without making a decision to, she turned and kissed him, smudging her carefully applied makeup and gripping him in a forceful embrace. If this was all they ever had it would be well worth it. No regrets.

At least she hoped not.

"And this is my grandmother." Simon smiled encouragingly. People milled around them in the royal enclosure, laughing and clinking glasses. Photographers were at a discreet distance. Mallets thwacked against balls somewhere in the background.

The queen looked so tiny up close. Ariella began to curtsey, but the queen stuck out her hand, so she took it. Cool and soft, the fingers closed around hers with surprising strength. "A pleasure to meet you, Miss Winthrop. Simon tells me you've never been to a polo match before." Steel-blue eyes peered into her very core.

"No, this is my first."

"Simon also informs me that President Morrow is your father." The queen's cool grip trapped her hands.

"Um, yes." Did she realize they'd never met, or even spoken? "Rather a surprise to both of us."

"Surprises do keep life interesting, don't they?"

"They do indeed."

The queen bombarded her with information about the various polo ponies, their breeding and track records and finer qualities. She was clearly skilled at holding the entire conversation with little participation from others. Ariella decided she'd work on that skill herself. It seemed a safe way to keep conversations on the right track.

Simon smiled and nodded and generally seemed delighted at how things were progressing. Ariella smiled and nodded while thinking, *Omigosh, I'm chatting about horses with the queen. And I don't know anything about horses. And I'm sleeping with her grandson.*

She was definitely ready for a Pimm's by the time a new arrival interrupted their conversation to greet Her Majesty. Simon procured her a large glass of the tea-colored drink with its floating mix of strawberries, apples, orange and cucumber. She knew the sweet taste hid a base of gin, so she sipped it gingerly, not wanting to find herself giggling and falling over in her stilettos as some of the younger guests were already in danger of doing.

Simon's younger brother Henry was at the center of the group of more rambunctious partygoers, and Ariella felt a sense of apprehension as Simon led her over to meet him.

As tall as Simon, but with curlier hair and bright blue eyes, the youngest prince had a reputation as a hard-partying playboy.

"I see you convinced her to step into the fray." He fixed his eyes on hers as he kissed her hand, which felt very awkward in front of the gathered crowd of guests. Young girls, spilling out of their expensive dresses, stared at her with curiosity.

"My brother, Henry, Ariella Winthrop." Simon made the introduction.

"I think everyone in the developed world knows who

Ms. Winthrop is. And she's even lovelier than her photographs."

What did you say to a comment like that? "It's nice to meet you."

"But is it? You haven't known me long enough to be sure."

"Don't scare Ariella." Simon was smiling. "She's just heard the pedigrees of the entire equine half of the polo team from Gran."

"I hope you showed a suitable degree of fascination. Gran is very suspicious of anyone who doesn't share her passion for horses."

"I freely admit that I know almost nothing about horses."

"I thought Montana was cowboy country?" Henry was obviously enjoying this.

"Some parts of it are, but not where I lived."

"I think Ariella would make a marvelous cowgirl." Simon slid his arm around her waist. She tried to keep a straight face. Did he really want to do that in front of all these people? She felt eyes boring into her from all directions. "But I intend to make her fall in love with England."

Henry raised an eyebrow. "He must be serious. Usually he can't wait to get on a plane and go somewhere looking for adventure."

"Ariella has me thinking about adventures closer to home."

Ariella could hardly believe her ears. He was all but declaring himself. Maybe this was some kind of ongoing joke between him and his brother. She had no idea how to react. "I like England very much."

"Well, thank goodness for that. There's one thing I can't change about myself, and that's my homeland." Simon squeezed her gently, which sent a ripple of confused emotions through her.

"I'm not sure you can change all that much else, either." Henry teased Ariella. "He's very bullheaded and opinionated."

"I am not." Simon shoved him gently. Ariella could see the brothers had a friendly sparring relationship, but that they cared for each other deeply. As someone who'd never had a sibling to rib her, she found their closeness touching.

"Ariella came up with the idea for an outdoor concert to raise money and awareness for World Connect."

"I like." Henry grinned. "The lawns in front of the Washington Monument would be a great spot."

"I agree." Ariella smiled. "No harm in aiming high."

"Especially when your dad is the president." Henry winked. "We royals aren't averse to a little nepotism when the occasion calls for it. It's how we pass on the throne, after all."

Ariella's stomach clenched slightly. Everyone seemed to assume that she had a relationship with her father, when nothing could be further from the truth.

"Uh-oh, here comes trouble." Henry's nod made Simon turn.

"Too true. Let's head it off at the pass." He turned and led Ariella away from Henry and his gaggle of blushing admirers toward a tall man in baggy tweeds, approaching fast through the knots of glamorous polo-goers.

"Your uncle?" The man's bushy brows sank low over slitted dark eyes and his cheeks were the florid pink of a smacked behind.

"Good old Uncle Derek. Here to pour gasoline on untroubled waters."

Derek marched up to Simon and launched into a conversation about the polo team, totally ignoring her. She counted the burst blood vessels in his cheeks and wondered if he intended to simply pretend she didn't exist.

"Uncle Derek, do hold your fire a moment so I can introduce you to my honored guest, Miss Ariella Winthop. Ariella, this is my mother's brother, Derek, the Duke of Aylesbury."

"Just visiting England, are you?" His haughty voice grated on her ears.

"Yes, I'm going back tomorrow."

"Oh." He turned back to Simon and launched into a tirade about poor sportsmanship at his shooting club. Simon caught her eye as he nodded and yessed his uncle. Ariella sagged with relief when Derek finally finished his monologue and sauntered off.

"He's irritating but harmless. I try to ignore him." Simon's whispered words in her ear made her giggle. "One thing you learn to do as a royal is present a united front. We don't need the public to know that behind closed doors sometimes we drive each other insane."

"Quite understandable." She admired his ability to play the role he'd been born to. Such responsibility and the strict code of conduct would be too much for a lot of people she knew. It almost invited rebellion and debauchery, but Simon handled his unique life with ease and good humor.

Which only made her adore him more.

There was a brief commotion as one of the players fell off and, unable to support weight on an injured ankle, was helped to a medical tent.

"Simon, we need you!" Two of the other players beckoned from their horses. "Hugh couldn't come today and Rupert's still down with the flu so we're short. You know Dom would be happy for you to ride his horses."

Simon glanced at Ariella, then back at them. "I can't, I'm afraid. It would be rude to desert my guest."

"Oh, that's okay," she protested. "I'm sure I can take care of myself for a few minutes." The game had been going on forever, it seemed. It must be nearly over. "You go ahead." She knew his side was winning and she didn't want everyone blaming her if things went south because Simon couldn't leave her side.

"You're a brick." He kissed her cheek softly, which made her gasp and glance around as he jogged off to change.

Great. Now she was adrift in unfamiliar waters. And her glass of Pimm's was empty, mint leaves clinging limply to the remains of the ice cubes. She decided to go off in search of another, and hope someone scored the winning goal while she was at it.

"Ariella." A voice startled her as she headed down the side of a marquee. She turned to find Simon's uncle Derek right behind her. "A word, if you please."

Actually, I don't please. But she didn't dare say it. She paused, still half turned toward the drinks tent.

"Simon's young and impressionable." Those frighteningly large salt-and-pepper brows waggled up and down. "Enthusiastic and charming but not terribly bright, I'm afraid."

Her mouth fell open. "I find him highly intelligent."

"I'm sure you do." He swigged from a glass of clear liquid. "A coronet has that effect on women. The fact remains that a dalliance with you could destroy his future."

"I hardly think that…" She didn't know what she was about to say but it didn't matter because Derek blazed ahead.

"We all know what happened the last time a member of the British royal family lost his head over an American. He abandoned his country and his duty in the name of love. Not because he wanted to, but because he knew it was an *absolute requirement*." His emphasis on the last two words was underscored with a hiss.

"Why?" Now she was curious to hear his answer.

"Because he knew she could not possibly fit in."

"I thought it was because the monarch can't marry a divorcée. For starters, Simon's not a monarch, or very likely to be one. And second, I'm not divorced." Her own boldness shocked her. Pimm's must be powerful stuff.

The monstrous brows shot up. "Times are different now, but not that different. Her Majesty holds very traditional views, and each of her grandchildren has been groomed from birth to follow a specific path. Simon will marry a member of the British nobility, and will raise his children here to be members of the British aristocracy. Lady Sophia Alnwick will be his future wife and the wedding invitations are all but printed. She'd be here with him today if she wasn't holding vigil at her esteemed father's deathbed. Within the next day or so she'll inherit all his lands and wealth and be the richest woman in England."

Ariella blinked. "I hardly think Simon needs to marry for money or prestige."

"Those two things are never a negative." Derek's beady black gaze chilled her. "You are a...a nobody. The illegitimate daughter of an American upstart who's clawed his way into a temporary position of power. Don't delude yourself that you can compete with the thousand-year history of the Alnwick family. Like his brother's, Simon's life path has been planned since birth. The estate he lives in, the so-called charity he's so enamored of, these are all part and parcel of his role. If you get your claws into him and cause him to do something foolish, he'll lose both of them."

"I don't believe you."

"No? The estate isn't his. It belongs to Her Majesty. That silly charity is funded almost entirely by the royal coffers. Simon's role in the family is a job like any other. His employment is contingent on Her Majesty's largesse, and can be rescinded at any time. Think about that when you kiss him."

He hissed the word *kiss,* and spittle formed on his bulbous lips. Then he turned and marched away. She wilted like the mint in her Pimm's. Was this true? Was Simon really a royal puppet whose strings could be cut at any time?

Part of her wanted to encourage him to tell them all to shove it and live his own life. Then she thought about how much he loved his home at Whist Castle. And how proud he was of the achievements of World Connect. Could she really be responsible for causing him to lose them both?

Her legs were shaking and her hand sweating around her glass. She hurried to the drinks tent and got another Pimm's, then walked around the perimeter of the royal enclosure, pretending to watch the match. She cheered wildly, heart pounding with pride and happiness, when Simon scored a goal. Then glanced around, wondering if she should have pretended more disinterest. He looked so dashing and handsome on top of the muscled bay horse, who listened to his every move and galloped for the ball as if its life depended on it.

"He's a fine player." The distinctive voice startled her.

"Yes, Your Majesty." The queen must have walked right up to her while her eyes were glued on Simon and she hadn't even noticed. Her attendants hovered at a discreet distance. "He obviously enjoys the game."

"Simon's been playing polo since he was about eleven. He'd already been riding for years at that point, of course. Do you ride?"

"No. I've never even sat on a horse. I suppose that seems

funny when I come from Montana, but we lived in town and I never had the chance."

"Ah. What did you do for entertainment in Montana?"

Ariella swallowed. This seemed dangerously personal. And she was to blame for bringing up her roots. "My dad used to take us to watch football games almost every weekend in season. And we went fishing at the lake."

"How nice." She didn't seem especially interested. And why should she be? "Do you plan to go back to Montana?"

"I have a business in Washington, D.C., so I'm not sure if I'll ever live in Montana again. Never say never, though."

"And when are you returning to Washington?" A hint of steel shimmered in her voice.

"Tomorrow, actually." Sadness mingled with relief. She'd have to leave Simon, but she wouldn't be stuck trying to make small talk with a monarch. "I was here on business. Simon's helped make it a wonderful trip."

She looked at the queen's face. She couldn't resist throwing in that last part.

"Simon tells me you're a party planner." The cool blue eyes had narrowed behind her glasses.

"Yes. I'm here to plan the Duke of Buckingham's wedding." She had no doubt the queen and the duke were old pals.

"How wonderful. Everyone's so happy to see him marrying Nicola at last. They've been chums almost since nursery school."

"I'll make sure it's an event to remember."

"I'm sure you will. Did Simon tell you he'll be getting married soon?"

She frowned. "What?"

The queen smiled sweetly. "A similar situation, really. A childhood friend who we all love. Perhaps he can get some wedding ideas from you."

Ariella's lung capacity seemed to shrink until she could hardly breathe. The queen was warning her off Simon. Telling her he was already spoken for and that she was not wanted on the voyage. A roar of clapping rose through the crowd and she joined in enthusiastically, though she wasn't even sure which team had scored a goal.

"I'm sure Simon's wedding will be an affair to remember," she managed at last.

"Indeed. Do have a good trip back to the States." The queen smiled thinly, then turned and walked slowly away.

Ariella felt like she'd just been slapped. She'd now been warned off Simon by two members of the royal family. They must feel quite threatened by her, which wasn't surprising given that Simon had allowed the press to get wind of their romance. Sophia Alnick was probably throwing a tantrum somewhere, too, if she was in on this whole aristocratic marriage scheme.

Standing there with her drink, she felt like a single tree in a tempest, while well-dressed people in big hats—she was hatless—swirled around her, going about their glamorous lives. Her role was to make those lives a little more glamorous by creating extravagant events for them, not to come play their own games with them. Clearly she was losing her grip on reality lately.

She counted the minutes until the match ended and Simon jumped down from his horse. He shared some congratulatory fist pumping with his teammates before jogging across the grass to her. "I hope everyone looked after you."

"Oh, yes."

He was even more handsome with his hair tousled and his chiseled face glowing with exertion. Shame he would never really be hers. "See? I told you they don't bite."

She didn't want to mention the tooth marks they'd left

on her psyche. Not while they were still here, at least. "I'm rather exhausted by all the excitement. Would it be okay if we left?" She certainly didn't want to find herself having to be polite to Uncle Derek, or even the queen, who'd practically shoved her toward her plane.

"Of course." He waved to a few people and escorted her to the car as if she really was the most important person there.

"Don't you need to say goodbye to the queen?" She didn't want to be blamed for him neglecting his royal duties.

"No worries. I'll be seeing her tomorrow after I take you to the airport."

"Oh." And why wouldn't he? She was his grandmother, after all. She probably wanted to go over wedding venue ideas, or discuss the ring he'd soon give to Sophia. Her heart sagged like a deflated balloon.

They talked about the game on the drive back to Whist Castle. Simon obviously loved his life here, surrounded by people who cared about him, and the excitement of his jet-set existence. He was born for it.

She wasn't.

They enjoyed a hearty dinner in the castle dining room, this time served by staff who were obviously trained to ignore the fact that he'd had a woman to stay for the weekend. They must know there was a connecting door between her room and Simon's, and she was pretty sure they knew she and Simon had been using it. It was embarrassing having so many people know her business. They'd all be whispering about her soon as Simon's last hurrah.

"You seem very thoughtful tonight." Simon spoke softly. They were still sitting at the dinner table, sipping coffee.

"Am I? I was just thinking about the Duke of Buckingham's wedding." There was some truth to it. This weekend had given her insight into the British upper crust that would help with the planning. "I hope I'm not being too dull."

"Impossible." His warm smile was so encouraging it almost melted her anxiety. "Let's go relax upstairs."

She gulped. How could she make love to him again, knowing that his family fully intended to keep them apart? "Okay." She'd always known this was never going to be a long-term thing. It was a crazy affair, something they'd both fallen into by accident.

He took her hand as they climbed the stairs, and the way he glanced at her sideways and squeezed her hand gently was so sweet and romantic, it stole her breath. Why did he have to be a prince? Why couldn't he have been a regular guy with an ordinary job and a house somewhere in the D.C. suburbs?

"You seem…worried." He closed the door to his room after they were both inside. The door to her own room was wide open. Apparently there was no pretense that they were sleeping apart.

"I am." It was hard not to be honest with him. He was such a straight shooter himself. "I'm going to miss you."

"Then we'll just have to make sure not to stay apart for too long." He gathered her in his arms and laid a warm kiss on her lips. Her anxiety started to unspool as she kissed him back.

"Yes." She said it but she didn't believe it. It would be better for both of them if they kissed and wandered back to their regular lives. Less media frenzy, less royal disapproval. Less fun.

Their kiss deepened until she had to come up for air. Simon's hands plucked at the zipper near her waist, and soon she was shimmying out of her dress and struggling

with his belt and undressing him. Even though everyone in
the outside world seemed to think he'd soon be marrying
Lady Sophia, right now she knew he wasn't interested in
anyone but her. Alone in this room they were two people
who cared about each other. It felt so good to shrug out of
the trappings of society and press her skin against his. His
naked body was so sturdy and capable. She had no doubt
he could leap tall buildings in a single bound if he wanted
to. She felt so confident in his presence, like together they
could accomplish anything. It would be hard to be back in
her D.C. apartment, alone.

Simon nibbled her jaw and neck, his breath hot and urgent. "I don't know what I'm going to do without you."

So she wasn't the only one thinking it. They slipped
under the bed clothes together. "You'll do what you did
before you met me. You know, climb mountains, jump
over waterfalls, that kind of thing."

"You're probably right. At least until my next trip to
D.C." He maneuvered himself on top of her and his erection nudged her belly.

She inhaled a shaky breath. "Who knows what will happen between now and then?" No doubt the royals would
warn him to stay away from her. If he had any sense, he'd
probably listen. She'd be busy with her own dramas—
meeting her father on national television, her frantic work
schedule, dodging photographers.

"Let's not think about the future. We don't want to
waste a single precious second of our last night together."
Arousal thickened his voice. He raised his hips and entered her.

Desire and relief crashed through her as she felt him
deep inside her. Sheer physical pleasure was a welcome
change from all the thinking and plotting and scrambling

she did during the day. Simon's powerful arms felt like the safest place to be in the whole world.

They moved together effortlessly, drawing to the brink of madness and back, as they tried to wring every last ounce of passion out of each other, only to find there was an inexhaustible well of it bubbling somewhere deep inside them.

When her orgasm came, Ariella wanted to cry. The feelings inside her were just too much. Desire and fear and pleasure and panic and wanting to stay right here in Simon's hot and hungry embrace until the world ended.

Simon gripped her tight, as if he was afraid she'd drift off into the night breeze. "Oh, Ariella," he whispered in her ear. She loved the way he said her name, with his formal sounding British accent and such conviction. She was sure no medieval knight ever serenaded his lady with such intensity.

She simply breathed, holding tight to the precious moments where she felt at peace, before she'd be spat back out into the world and have to fend for herself.

In the morning an alarm sounded, reminding them both that she had a plane to catch in a little over four hours. It was odd that you could be sleeping in a royal palace, with a prince, no less, then have to battle your way into coach and cram your bags into the overhead bin and hope your neighbor didn't drool on you while he slept.

She wanted to laugh, but nothing seemed too funny right now.

"Did you like my family?" Simon's odd question came out of nowhere.

It startled her into a fib. "They were very nice."

"Except Uncle Derek." His voice sounded curious.

"Yes, except him."

He sat up. "Did he say something to you?"

She hesitated for a moment. Why hadn't she told him about this already? She didn't want to spoil their last night together. And she knew it would upset him. "Kind of." Simon took her hand and peered into her face. She wanted to run from his thoughtful and caring expression, not hurt his feelings by telling him what his uncle had said to her. "I have to get ready."

"What did he say?"

"Oh, nothing really." She tried to get up, but he held her hand firm.

"I don't believe you. Come on, word for word or I'll have to start in with the medieval torture techniques." He acted like he was going to tickle her. But neither of them laughed.

"He said you're going to marry Sophia Alnwick soon."

"Which you already know is not true."

"And he reminded me of what happened the last time a British royal got involved with an American."

"You're hardly Wallace Simpson."

"I told him that. Not that it matters, anyway, since we're barely even dating. It was silly. I didn't think it was worth mentioning."

"Did anyone else say anything?"

"Not really. Though the queen did seem fairly interested in when I was going back to the States. I suspect they'll all be glad to see the back of me so you can go back to dating some nice, suitable English girls." She smiled and tried to sound jokey. That was what would happen after all.

But Simon's face was like stone. "I'll have a talk with them." He frowned. "I'm sorry they made you feel uncomfortable."

"I was fine, really. It was fun. I've never been to a polo match before and I loved watching you play."

"I shouldn't have left you alone. I'll sort them out."

"There's no need, really!" Her voice sounded too loud. Would they tell him what they'd told her? That he'd lose Whist Castle and his charity if he dared not to toe the royal party line? "I need to get dressed and throw my stuff back in my bag. And do you have the number for a taxi?"

"A taxi!" He wrapped his arms around her and hugged her tight. "There's no way anyone but me is driving you to that airport. And it'll be a miracle if I don't make you deliberately miss your plane."

"Then my partner, Scarlet, will kill me. She's been holding down the fort by herself all week."

"She can't kill you if she can't find you." He raised a brow and mischief twinkled in his eyes again.

"She can send out a hit man. They're good at tracking people. They can probably trace my cell phone."

"They'd have to get past the palace guards." He kissed her face and cheeks and lips. She shivered, hot pleasure rising inside her. "It can be handy living in a fortress."

"I see that." Her hands roamed over the muscle of his back. "I think I could get used to it." It was so easy to talk to him and tease him. He never made her feel like he was a prince and she was a commoner. With him she felt they were on the same team and could take on the world together.

The alarm sounded again. She pushed him back, very reluctantly, and leaped out of bed. "Duty calls."

"Being in the army I know all about that, so I suppose I'll have to go along with it."

They dressed and had a quick breakfast, then Simon drove her to Heathrow. They kissed in the car where no one could see, but he insisted on walking her into the terminal. She saw a photographer's flash out of the corner of her eye as they said a chaste goodbye.

Move along, she wanted to say. *There's nothing to see*

here. She felt numb as she checked her bag and moved through customs. Would he really come to D.C. to see her? Or would the queen and Uncle Derek make him give her up and turn his attention back to his royal duties?

Somehow she had to go from the most intense and wonderful romance of her life to…nothing. Maybe she'd never see him again except on the pages of a glossy magazine. She sank into her airplane seat feeling hollow and deflated.

Until she checked her phone and discovered that she was about to finally meet her famous father.

Eight

A brief text from Liam Crowe, the head of ANS, told her the taping was scheduled for Tuesday, only two days away, and everyone at the network was scrambling to pull it together. Ariella had barely arrived home and unpacked before Francesca, Liam's wife, came over to help her prep for the taping.

"It seems shallow to ask, but what do you think I should wear?" They both sat at her kitchen table, sipping herbal tea. Her nerves were firing like bullets. "I usually wear black but I've heard that doesn't look good on video. It disappears or something. I don't want it to vanish and leave me stark naked on national television."

Francesca's bold laugh filled the room. "It looks a bit flat, that's all. But colors do usually work better. Let's go look at your wardrobe."

They walked into the bedroom. Ariella opened her closet door sheepishly. The apartment was old, from an era when people had maybe five to ten outfits. Her collection of clothes looked ready to burst out and start running.

"How do you find anything in here?"

"My first boss used to have a sign on her desk that read, *'This is not a mess on my desk, it's a wilderness of free association.'* I took it as inspiration."

"It's a wilderness, all right." Still, Francesca dove boldly in and pulled out a knee-length red sheath. "Red portrays confidence."

"That I don't feel. I think I should go low-key."

"You? You're practically a princess. How about this royal blue?" She held up a matching top and skirt in an intense shade.

"I am sooo not practically a princess. Believe me. I was way out of my league with his family."

"You met the queen?" Francesca grabbed her arm.

She nodded. "We made small talk. It was scary." Ariella reached in for a quiet gray jacket and skirt. "How about this?"

"Way too mousy." Francesca shoved it back. "I can't believe you met the queen. I love her. She's so old-fashioned."

"Exactly. The kind of person who's horrified by the prospect of her grandson dating an Amerrrrican." She managed to roll her *R*s. Then sighed. "He's sweet but it's one of those things with no future."

"I'll have to read your tea leaves when we're done picking your outfit."

"Does that work when you're using a tea bag?"

"It does require more creativity, but I have plenty of that."

"Let's just stay focused on getting me through this taping in one piece. How about this lilac number?"

Francesca surveyed the dress. "Perfect. Fresh and young, yet sophisticated and worldly."

"I'm glad that's settled. Will I get to meet the pres— I mean, my father, before the taping starts?"

Francesca hesitated. "Liam and I did talk about that. He wants you to meet for the first time on air, for maximum dramatic impact. I told him this isn't a primetime special—well, it is—but it's your real life. If you don't like the idea of meeting him under the studio lights, I'll beg and plead until he gives in."

"Don't worry about it. I don't mind meeting him on camera. In a way it might help as I'll have to keep a lid on my emotions."

"Oh, don't do that. It's bad for ratings." Francesca winked.

"Liam would rather have me blubbering and calling him Daddy?"

"Absolutely."

She blew out a breath. "Yikes. That's not really me. I'm known for being calm under pressure. I'm afraid I won't give good TV."

"You just be yourself, and we'll let Liam worry about the ratings."

Ariella's usually calm demeanor was trembling. Her hands kept shaking as she tried to apply her mascara. Her lips quivered as she smoothed on her lipstick. Even her hair seemed jumpy. In seventeen minutes—not that she was counting—she'd be sitting on a sound stage with the man who shared half her DNA. She wasn't that nervous about the television cameras, or even the audience of millions that would supposedly be tuning in. She was nervous about what she'd see when she looked into Ted Morrow's face.

Would his expression encourage her to build a relationship that could shape the rest of her life? Or would he be wearing that mask of genial competence that had helped him clinch the election? She knew that mask. She wore it herself a lot. In fact, she planned on wearing it tonight.

She hoped that this meeting might be the start of a relationship between them, but she was keeping her hopes in check since he didn't know her well enough to trust her. He might not want to get close to anyone new. He was in a position of power and influence that made him strangely vulnerable. He probably didn't want to share intimacies and feelings with a stranger who might turn around and repeat them to the press, or even to her friends. Still, she knew she'd be disappointed if she didn't feel even a little bit closer to him after tonight.

"We're on in five!" The perky production assistant stuck her head around the corner. "Are you ready?"

"Ready as I'll ever be." She stood up on shaky legs and smoothed out the skirt of her lavender dress.

"You can come sit in the green room. The president is chatting with Liam so you won't meet him until we're on air."

"It's going to be totally live?" There'd been some back and forth about whether it would be taped and then edited, but the ANS producer had reassured her that if it was live she was actually more in control of the final output than if it ended up in the hands of directors and editors. Apparently live was also better for ratings.

"Yup. No delay. No one expects either of you to start cursing or doing anything else that needs to be tweaked before it goes out." The PA squeezed her arm. "You'll be great. Just remember not to talk too fast and try not to look at the cameras."

"Okay." She said it to reassure herself as much as the PA. What if she froze and couldn't speak? What if she passed out in a dead faint? Whatever happened would be seen live by millions of curious onlookers.

She followed the PA into the green room, which wasn't green at all but mostly gray and had two sofas and some chairs. A jug of water, glasses and a basket of muffins. She certainly didn't have any appetite. She sat on one of the sofas and smiled weakly.

The PA looked at a sheet of paper in her hand. "Barbara Carey will be going in first to introduce you, then the president will come in." Celebrity journalist Barbara Carey was known for her ability to make all her interviewees cry. They'd probably picked her just for that reason. No matter what happened, Ariella was sure she wouldn't cry. All she had to do was stay calm, be polite and survive the half-hour ordeal.

A light went on near the door marked Studio C. "Has the show started?"

"Yup, they're taping. Get ready." She ushered Ariella over to the door, and opened it quietly. The lights blinded her as she stepped onto a big sound stage with cameras on all sides. Barbara Carey was sitting in a set that looked a bit like a living room, with soft chairs and a potted plant. There was an empty chair on either side of her. In a few seconds she'd be sitting in one of those looking at her father.

Her heart clenched and unclenched and she tried to keep her breathing steady.

Barbara Carey's voice filled the air. "…a young woman who's been plucked out of obscurity and thrust onto the world stage by the startling revelation that her father is none other than the president of the United States. Ariella Winthrop." The PA had maneuvered her just outside the scene, so she plunged forward. Barbara stood and she shook her hand, then she sat in the seat indicated. Where was the president? She fought the urge to look around to see if he was standing offstage somewhere.

"Did you have any idea at all that your father was Ted Morrow?" Up close Ariella could see that Barbara Carey was wearing a tremendous amount of makeup, including long false eyelashes.

"Not until I read it in the papers like everyone else."

"Had your parents told you that you were adopted?" She leaned in, sincerity shining in her famous blue eyes.

"Oh, yes, I always knew that I was adopted. They told me my mother was unmarried and too young to provide for me and that she gave me up so that I could have a better life." Her thoughts strayed to Eleanor, so nervous and desperate to hide from the limelight. She'd rather die than be here on this stage.

"And did you ever hope to meet your birth parents?"

"I didn't." She frowned. People probably thought it shallow, but it was the truth. "I considered my adoptive parents to be my mother and father."

"But they died in a tragic accident. Surely you must have wondered about the man and woman that gave you life?"

"Maybe I didn't let myself wonder. I didn't want to try to replace my mother and father in any way." This was turning out to be more of an interview than she expected, and making her nervous. She wished they'd hurry up and bring Ted Morrow out. She probably wasn't giving them the emotional yearning they were hoping for. "But I'm glad of the opportunity to meet my father."

No one knew she'd already met her mother. She'd sworn to keep it a secret, and she'd stand by her promise.

"And you shall." Barbara Carey stood. "Let me introduce you to your father, President Ted Morrow."

A hush fell over the room as she rose to her feet, peering into the darkness just beyond the studio lights. The familiar face of the president emerged, tall, handsome, smiling. He looked at her and their eyes met. Her breath stuck in her lungs as he thrust out his hand and she took it. His handshake was firm and warm and she hoped it would go on forever. His eyes were so kind, and as she looked into them she saw them brimming with emotion. "Hello, Ariella. I'm very happy to meet you." His voice was low and gruff.

Her heart beat faster and faster and her breathing grew shallow. "I'm very pleased to meet you, too." The polite words did nothing to express the deep well of emotion suddenly rushing inside her.

His pale blue eyes locked with hers, and she could see shadows of thoughts flickering behind them. "Oh, my." His murmur almost seemed to have come from her own mouth. Overwhelmed, their hands still clasped together, they stared at each other for a long time that seemed agonizingly short and then she felt his arms close around her back.

The breath rushed from her lungs as she hugged him back and held him with the force of twenty-eight years of unexpressed longing. She could feel his chest heaving as he held her tight. Tears fell from her eyes into the wool of his suit and she couldn't stop them. It was too much. Feelings she'd never anticipated rocked her to her core. When they finally parted she was blinking and pretty sure that she wouldn't be able to talk if someone asked her a question. The president's—her father's—eyes were wet with tears and his face still looked stunned.

He helped her to one of the seats, then took his place in the other, on the opposite side of Barbara Carey, who tactfully remained silent, letting the moment speak for itself. At last the interviewer drew in a breath. "It's been a long time coming." She looked from one of them to the other.

Ariella's father—it didn't feel crazy to call him that

now, which didn't really make any sense, but then none of this did—stared straight at her. "I had no idea you existed." His voice was breathless, as if he was talking just to her, not to Barbara Carey, or the cameras, or the viewers.

"I know," she managed. She'd known he existed, of course, but not who he was.

"Your parents have obviously done a wonderful job of raising you. I've learned of all your accomplishments, and how well you've handled the avalanche of events these last few months."

She smiled. "Thanks."

"I should have met with you before now but I was foolish enough to take the advice of strategists who wanted to wait until we knew the truth from the DNA testing." His eyes softened. "I was a fool. I only have to look at you to know you're my daughter. And you have your mother's eyes."

Those same eyes filled with tears again, and she reached for one of the tissues from a box that had miraculously appeared on a small coffee table in front of them. Suddenly she could see herself in the jut of his cheekbone and the funny way he wrinkled his nose. They'd been living their lives often only a few buildings apart here in D.C. but might have never met.

"I suppose we have to be grateful for the nosey journalists who uncovered the truth." She said it to him, then turned to Barbara Carey. "Or we might have lived the rest of our lives without ever meeting."

"We have a lot of lost time to make up for." Ted Morrow leaned forward. "I'd like very much to get to know you."

"I'd like that, too." Her heart swelled until she thought it might burst. "I've been longing to meet you since I first learned you were my father. It's not easy getting an appointment with the president."

He shook his head. "I've been anxious to meet you, too. It's usually a mistake to let other people tell you how to run your life, and it's one I won't make again. I have a strange feeling we'll find we have a lot in common."

She smiled. "I've wondered about that. And I'd like to learn more about your life in Montana."

Something flickered across Ted Morrow's face. Maybe he was thinking back to his high school days, where he'd become involved with Eleanor. She wondered how he felt about being deceived for all these years. Would he forgive Eleanor for keeping her secret?

"I had a wonderful childhood in Montana. And I was very much in love with your mother." He spoke with force, eyes still shining with emotion. "It's been a strange journey since then, for sure. Who knows how different it would have been if she'd told me she was pregnant with you?"

"You might not be sitting here as president of the United States," suggested Barbara. "Your life might have taken a different course."

"I might have accepted the assistant manager position I was offered at Willey's Tool and Die." He chuckled. "They paid time and a half for weekends."

"But you had bigger dreams." Barbara tilted her head. "You'd just accepted a scholarship to attend Cornell University."

"I wanted to get out of my small pond and see if I could swim in a larger one." Then his eyes fixed on hers again. "I never intended to abandon Ellie."

Barbara Carey leaned toward him. "Ellie is Eleanor Albert, your high school sweetheart?"

"Yes. I wrote her letters and we'd made plans to spend the summer together." He frowned. "Then one day she stopped responding to my letters. She didn't answer the phone. Her mother hung up on me." He shook his head. "I guessed that she'd met someone else. I had no idea she'd been bundled out of town to hide a pregnancy."

"And you never saw her again." Barbara's famous voice added drama to the pronouncement.

He looked right at her. "Never. I've certainly thought about her over the years. Wondered where she was and hoped she was happy."

"But you never married anyone else."

"I guess I just never met anyone I loved as much as Ellie."

His usually granite-hard features were softened with emotion. Ariella's heart ached at the thought that Eleanor—Ellie—was out there and deathly afraid of him. Thinking he'd be angry and would hate her for her choice to keep her secret. She vowed that once she got to know him she'd convince Eleanor to meet him in person.

"Well, we have a surprise for you, President Morrow."

He lifted a brow. "I'm not sure how many more surprises I can take. It's been quite a year for them."

Barbara stood and peered off into the darkness beyond the studio lights, and both Ariella and her father instinctively stood as well. "It wasn't easy to convince her, but I'm happy to tell you that Eleanor is here with us tonight."

Ariella gasped. She tried to make out her mother's face but it was too hard to see. She glanced at Ted Morrow, but he simply looked shocked. At last she made out Liam Crowe, the head of ANS, walking toward them with Eleanor on his arm. Her hair was carefully coiffed, and she wore a simple burgundy dress, and looked young and pretty, and very, very nervous.

Her eyes were riveted on Ted Morrow like she'd seen a ghost.

"Ellie." The president breathed her name like a prayer. "It's really you."

Blinking, she walked into the glare of the lights. "Hello, Ted." Her voice was tiny, barely audible. He enveloped her in the same bear hug he'd greeted Ariella with, but there was something…tentative about the way he held her.

Stage hands quietly appeared with a chair for her to sit on, next to Ariella, who she greeted nervously.

Barbara leaned toward Ted. "I have to tell you that Eleanor approached us. She had heard of the special from Ariella, and she decided it was time to face you and tell her side of the story."

Ted stared at Eleanor in a daze as if he couldn't believe she was really here.

"Ariella and I met in London." She spoke quietly. "Meeting her meant so much to me. I don't suppose I realized how much I gave up until I saw her beautiful face and talked with her. After that I knew I had to face you again, too, Ted."

"I never knew what happened to you. I pestered your mother for years but she never told me. She said you'd gone to live abroad."

"It was true. I met my husband, married him and moved to Ireland all within a year of giving birth to Ariella. It seemed easier for everyone if I just disappeared."

"It wasn't easier for me," Ted protested. "Why didn't you tell me? You know I'd have married you."

She looked at him in silence, her lip trembling. "I knew that's what you'd do. That you'd give up your dreams to do the right thing. I couldn't let you do that."

"Ellie." Tears filled his eyes. "Maybe there were other things that were more important to me than building a big career."

"I'm so sorry." Eleanor's voice was higher. She was beginning to look as if she regretted coming. Ariella grabbed her hand and squeezed it. "Looking back I can see I made a terrible mistake. I was in a panic. My family said that the scandal of an unwed pregnancy would ruin your prospects. It was a different time. I was young and stupid and alone. I didn't know what to do and I followed bad advice."

"The important thing is that we're all here today." Ted Morrow's voice sounded presidential for the first time since he'd come on set. "We've all done things we'd do differently if we had the chance to do them over again. Instead of looking back and saying 'if only,' I suggest that we embrace the present."

"Well said," chimed in Barbara. "And we here at ANS are thrilled to be a part of bringing you all together again."

After the taping, they filed into the green room. Ariella felt shell-shocked. They'd all watched an edited montage of childhood photographs and background interviews and answered a few more questions. She was relieved it was over but also anxious to make sure she didn't miss the opportunity to get to know her father and mother better.

Ted and Eleanor stood together, awkwardly silent, staring at each other. She wondered if she should say something to break the ice, but then she wondered if it wasn't ice but something far warmer and maybe she should stay out of the way.

"You haven't changed at all." The president's usually commanding voice sounded gruff with emotion.

"You, either. Though the gray at your temples makes you look more distinguished." Eleanor's eyes sparkled. "I wasn't at all surprised to learn that you were running for president. I even obtained an absentee ballot for the first time so I could vote for you."

Ted laughed. "It was a close race. I'm glad of the help." He looked like he wanted to say so much more. He took her hands. "I know you did what you thought was best."

He spoke softly, as if they were all alone, though Ariella stood only a few feet away and production staff moved in the background.

"It doesn't seem that way now, but you know what they say about hindsight."

"I never loved anyone else." Ted's soft words shocked Ariella. She felt embarrassed to be eavesdropping, and wanted to disappear. But she knew how hard it was to engineer this meeting in the first place and who knew when she'd get another chance to spend time with her father. "I probably shouldn't tell you that. I know you were married."

"Greg was a good man." Ellie didn't seem so nervous and skittish anymore. Being in Ted's presence seemed to calm her. "He was always so kind to me and we shared a good life together, even though we were never blessed with children."

"I'm sorry to hear that he died."

"Yes, it was very sudden and unexpected." Their gazes were still locked on each other and they held hands as if afraid circumstances might suddenly tug them apart again.

It made her think of Simon. Circumstances certainly conspired to keep them apart. In fact it was odd that they'd ever met and managed to forge a few moments of intimacy. Some things just weren't meant to be. She was almost at peace about it. It had been a fun fling, a wonderful whirlwind romance, and now she needed to get back to her regular life—whatever regular was these days—and try to forget about him.

"Do you think we could…have dinner together?" Ted Morrow asked with a touchingly hopeful expression.

"I'd like that very much." Eleanor glowed. She looked so young and lovely standing there with Ted. Ariella would barely have recognized her as the white-lipped, anxious woman who'd met her in their secret London hiding place. "We have a lot to catch up on."

They both seemed to suddenly remember her. "You will join us, won't you?" Ted reached out and took Ariella's hand, so that they were all linked. "It would mean so much to me to finally get to know you after all these years."

"I'd be thrilled."

The dinner was very emotional. Their happiness at meeting was thickened with sadness at all the things they'd missed sharing together. Ariella arrived home feeling literally sick with exhaustion, emotional and physical. She'd had her phone turned off since before the taping, and when she finally turned it on she saw that Simon had left a message.

"Great news. I've managed to engineer a series of meetings in D.C. next week. I'd like to put in my application now to take you out for dinner on Tuesday. Call me."

Her heart constricted, partly with the familiar thrill of hearing his voice, and partly with the ugly knowledge that she needed to start weaning herself off him, not getting excited about dinners. Feeling dizzy, she lay down on her sofa, clutching the phone to her chest. She listened to another message from her partner, Scarlet, asking her to call and fill her in on the details. She decided that could wait until tomorrow because Scarlet had probably watched the taping like everyone else.

Her phone rang and she didn't have the energy to come up with a strategy, so she answered it. "Were you ever going to call me, or what?"

"Hi, Scarlet." Her voice sounded far away, like it belonged to someone else. "I'm wiped out."

"I bet you are. That was quite a live reunion. I do believe your parents are still madly in love with each other."

"Was that obvious on television, too? I felt like a third wheel."

"You don't sound good. Are you okay?"

"I'm feeling a little queasy. I'm probably dehydrated or something." They'd been out for a big fancy dinner but she'd found herself barely able to eat. "And I need a good night's sleep."

"All right then. Don't forget we have the Morelli meeting in the morning."

Ariella groaned. She'd totally forgotten they were meeting with the extended Morelli clan to plan a huge fiftieth wedding anniversary. "Ten o'clock, right."

"Call me if you're not up for it, okay? I can handle it."

"I'll be fine."

But she wasn't.

When her alarm went off at eight her comforter felt like a lead blanket. Her eyes didn't want to open. "Coffee. I need coffee," she tried to convince herself. But the moment she managed to get her feet on the floor, a wave of nausea hit her.

Her phone rang on the dresser on the far side of the room, and she leaped to her feet to go answer it. Or at least she tried, but her ankles didn't seem capable of holding weight so she found herself flopping back onto the bed, her breath coming in unsteady gasps.

After about five minutes of deep breathing she got the nausea under control, and managed to walk like a zombie to her phone. Scarlet had called again, so she dialed back without even listening to her message. "You know what you said about doing the meeting without me?"

"Not a problem. You sound terrible."

Her voice did sound rather raspy. "I must have come down with something. I'd better lie in bed for a bit."

"You stay right there and I'll keep you posted on everything that happens."

Ariella stayed in bed all morning. Every time she tried to do something useful the room started spinning or her stomach began to heave. She hadn't been sick in so long she'd forgotten how miserable it was. It was probably from all the stress and anxiety leading up to the TV special. She probably needed a day or two in bed to recover.

Not that she had time for that. She had phone calls to make, menus and décor to approve and clients to meet. But maybe she could lie down for a few minutes first.

Ariella awoke with a start to the sound of the doorbell. A quick glance at the clock revealed she'd been asleep for four hours. She staggered to the door and opened it.

Scarlet stood on the threshold with a concerned look in her face. "I brought some chicken soup." She thrust forward a container from the expensive bistro around the corner. "It has antibacterial properties."

"What if it's a virus?" Ariella couldn't resist teasing her.

"Ah, so you're not as sick as I thought. Let's put it in bowls anyway. I need to grab some lunch before I meet with the manager of that new venue near the river."

"I feel a lot better now. I think I've just been burning the candle too fast lately."

"And Prince Simon has been helping you do it." Scarlet lifted a brow. "But you had a few days to recover from your British romp before the taping."

"Not enough, I guess." She led Scarlet into the kitchen and pulled out two bowls and two spoons. "I usually fight everything off but maybe it's catching up with me. At least I made it through the televised reunion."

"What's he like?" Scarlet poured the soup into both bowls. "The president, I mean."

Ariella paused. "I liked him." She looked right at

Scarlet. "I mean, I liked him before, enough to vote for him—which is lucky, I guess—but he's very genuine and unpretentious in real life. You could tell he found the whole situation rather overwhelming, and that really touched me."

"I saw you guys both weeping."

"And I'd sworn I wouldn't do that." She grabbed a paper towel and wiped up some spilled drops of soup. "I can usually put a lid on any emotion."

"I know. I've seen you in action with the nuttiest clients and guests."

"But the whole thing blew me away. He's my father. We have the same genes. We probably have some of the same likes and dislikes, and he has the same funnily shaped earlobes as I do."

Scarlet peered at her earlobes. "Cool."

"It's frightening to think that I might never have met him. Simon was so right that this is a big life-changing opportunity for me."

"I hear ya. We can plan some White House parties now." Scarlet winked.

"You know what I mean. I have a new set of parents. They'll never replace my parents who raised me, of course, but we'll have new experiences together. We've already made plans to go up to his house in Maine for a few days in the fall."

"Without consulting me?" Scarlet put her hands on her hips in mock indignation. "Just because your daddy's the president and you're dating a prince doesn't mean we're not still partners."

They both laughed. Ariella shook her head. "What next?" A wave of nausea rolled through her. "I need to sit down."

Scarlet followed her into the living room, brow furrowed with concern. "Have some soup." She held out the bowl. "Have you eaten anything at all today?"

Ariella shook her head. Her throat slammed shut at the sight of the soup. "I have no appetite."

"Maybe you're pregnant." Scarlet smiled. She was kidding.

"Sure, if Simon and I had sex."

"You have though, haven't you?" She leaned in. "Even though you won't share the juicy details."

"Barely a week ago. I couldn't possibly be pregnant."

"It only takes one time. And my mom said she started feeling symptoms right away. She took a test and it was positive less than two weeks later."

"We used condoms." Ariella's nausea was getting worse. Scarlet was kidding, wasn't she?

"Don't they have a five percent failure rate?"

"What?" Her grip tightened on her unused spoon.

"That's why most people use something else as well. Still, you're probably not pregnant. You've had a lot on your plate." Scarlet leaned back into the armchair and spooned some soup into her mouth. "Don't worry about it."

Ariella stared at the bowl of soup Scarlet had placed on the coffee table. There was no way she could eat that. There was also no way she could be pregnant.

No. Way. It simply wasn't possible.

Was it?

Nine

Simon paused outside the building where his meeting was to take place and punched Ariella's number into his phone. She was proving very elusive since she'd gone home to D.C. If he were more sensitive he might think she was trying to avoid him. The phone rang, and he leapt to his feet when he heard her tentative, "Hello."

"How are you?" He managed not to ask where she'd been. Didn't want to seem too oppressive.

"Um, fine. How are you?" She sounded oddly formal.

"I'd be a lot better if you were here." He glanced around the busy London street. His imagination wanted to picture her darting along the pavement as she had been when he'd followed her on her secret assignation to meet her mother. "I can't wait to see you next week."

"Yeah." Her voice was barely audible. "Me, either."

"Are you okay?"

"I'm fine." The words shot into his ear so fast he almost jumped. "Great. Really busy with work. You know how it goes."

"Absolutely." There was so much he wanted to say to her but he knew now wasn't the right time. He'd probably come on too strong already, and he was pretty sure that introducing her to his family had been a tactical error. He'd been so sure they'd be bowled over by her charms like he was that he couldn't wait to get the introductions out of the way. Henry had been right. Poor Ariella. There was hardly anyone on earth who wasn't intimidated by the queen, and Uncle Derek was a force of nature akin to a sinkhole. He should have introduced her to one or two family members on a one-on-one basis and let her get to know them before plunging her into their midst. "I did rather shove you into the middle of things here. I could tell you were a bit dazed by your visit."

She laughed. "Was it that obvious? I was way out of my league."

"You were fantastic. I'm sure they'll adore you when they get to know you." He'd caught a lot of flack for bringing her to such a public event with no warning. Pictures of the pair of them had been all over the papers for the next week and there'd been a lot of flapping about suitable relationships and time to settle down and stop playing the field.

He tried to ignore the naysayers. You couldn't hold a sensible argument with fifteen hundred years of tradition so he'd learned to pick his battles and go about his business. If they wanted him to settle down, fine. But not with Sophia Alnwick. And if not her, then why not a fun, sexy, intelligent American girl? He generally preferred to just do stuff and explain it afterward, not get people all fired up over something that might not happen. "I can't wait to see you." Her face hovered in his mind all the time. He wished he could reach out and squeeze her. Traffic weaved along Regent Street in front of him, but time seemed to be standing still until he could see Ariella again.

"Me, neither." She didn't sound her usual self. Maybe she was in a room with other people, or rushing between appointments.

"I miss you."

"I miss you, too." For the first time she seemed to be speaking directly to him. "But I'm worried we're getting into something that's…too big."

He froze. "That's impossible." Then he realized that he was pushing things along the way he tended to, and he tried to rein himself back. "We're dating. That's a perfectly normal thing for two healthy adults to do, don't you think?"

"Well, yes, but…we're both in the public eye. And your family, I don't think they…"

"Don't you worry about what they think. Sometimes they need a little convincing but believe me, I have years of experience in that department."

"I don't want things to move too fast."

"I know. I've been telling myself to slow down. Sometimes I'm like a steam locomotive in motion, but I'm putting the brakes on, I promise you." He was running late for his meeting. "When I get to Washington, we'll do everything so slow it will be downright kinky." He glanced about, suddenly remembering he was in a public street.

She chuckled, but again, it wasn't her usual enthusiastic laugh. She must be getting cold feet now that they were apart. Which only made him more impatient to get there and warm them up for her.

"I've got a board meeting for UNICEF, so I have to go, but I'll talk to you soon," he said after a pause.

"Great. Thanks for calling." She sounded a bit like she couldn't wait to hang up. He was tempted to call her on it, then reminded himself not to be pushy.

"You're more than welcome." Telling her he loved her would be waaaay too much pressure, even if he was convinced it might be true. That could wait for a more intimate moment, preferably one where no one but Ariella was in earshot.

Ariella hung up the phone with her gut churning. In the last three days since Scarlet had planted the idea in her mind, she'd become more and more convinced that she was pregnant. She hadn't paid much attention to her menstrual cycle before, but based on the last period she could remember, she was due for another one, and it wasn't showing up.

Talking to Simon and trying to pretend everything was normal was agony. She could barely get words out of her mouth, let alone make polite conversation. How would his snooty family feel about the exciting surprise of an unplanned pregnancy? She'd bet that wouldn't go over too well.

If she was pregnant, of course. There was no way to be sure until she took a test. Scarlet had brought one over for her yesterday and told her to take it whenever she felt ready. It sat on the shelf in the bathroom, in its unopened white-and-pink box, mocking her.

Was she too chicken to find out the truth? Possibly. If she confirmed a pregnancy, she'd have to deal with how to tell people. Scarlet, for a start. She had enough money saved to take some time off work, but you didn't run a small business with someone then announce that you'd need a year of maternity leave. Then there was Simon….

She walked slowly into the bathroom and looked at the test. Picked up the box and read the directions. It sounded easy. Maybe she wasn't pregnant? Maybe the nausea was just from stress and exhaustion as she'd first suspected. Or maybe she'd eaten something funny.

Her nipples had become very sensitive, but that could happen when she was expecting her period. Same with the sudden swings of emotion that made her weep over television coverage of the fund drive at a local dog shelter. She could simply be losing her mind. People had cracked under less extreme circumstances than she'd found herself in lately.

Her stomach contracted as she picked up the box and ripped it open. She was a big girl and could handle the consequence of her choices. She'd willingly had sex with Simon, and sex could lead to pregnancy. Everyone knew that.

But for some reason it hadn't crossed her mind even once during those steamy nights in Simon's bed. In his castle.

Go on. Do it.

She picked up the stick and followed the directions, waiting the exact amount of time listed while watching the long hand of her watch. If she were pregnant, a line would appear. If she weren't the little circle would remain blank. She'd never wanted to see a blank space so much in her life. Her eyes started to play tricks on her during the agonizing wait, so she hid the stick under a tissue while the time was passing. When she reached the full five minutes she held her breath and lifted the tissue….

To see a thick pink line bisecting the white circle.

"Oh." She said the word aloud, and startled herself. Then she ran from the room as if she could run away from the whole situation. Which, of course, followed her. Apparently—and she still couldn't believe it—there was a baby growing inside her belly, right now. She glanced down at the waistband of her jeans. Her snug T-shirt sat against a totally flat stomach. Though of course at this stage the baby probably wasn't larger than her pinkie nail.

Suddenly she felt dizzy and plunged for the sofa. How could it all happen this fast? She'd slept with Simon for the first time less than two weeks ago and now her entire life was about to change forever. It didn't make sense.

She jumped out of her skin when the phone rang. A quick glance at the number revealed that it was Francesca. Normally she shared everything with her. She'd even taken her mother's very private letter to show Francesca when it had first arrived and she needed to share it with someone. But her friend was now madly in love with the head of the most powerful television in network in the country, and this was quite possibly the scoop of the century. What if Francesca tried to convince her to announce it on air? After meeting her father for the first time in front of the entire country, it seemed anything was possible and her own privacy, even her feelings, were of little importance.

She let the call go to voicemail, as guilt trickled through her. More secrets and subterfuge. She wouldn't tell Simon until he got here. It wasn't the kind of news you should break over the phone and she'd see him in a few days. She'd have to tell Scarlet right away, especially since the nausea came and went in waves and she wasn't sure how useful she'd be on the floor at events if she might have to rush to the ladies' every few minutes.

And then there were the reporters. The TV special had reignited interest and she'd had a harrowing couple of days trying to smile and answer journalists' questions every time she left the house. The creepy bearded guy who practically camped on her block had been joined by a few other camera-laden competitors, all vying for a money shot of her doing something newsworthy, like having a bad hair day. Maybe she could sneak away and run off to Ireland? It had worked for her mom, though of course she'd had her baby before she left.

The similarity in their circumstances smacked Ariella across the face. On instinct she picked up the phone and dialed the number of her mother's D.C. hotel room. Ted Morrow had persuaded Ellie to stay in D.C. at least until the end of the month, so they could all have a chance to get to know each other again. Ellie's now-familiar soft voice answered.

"It's Ariella." A strange wave of relief rushed through her, which was crazy as she'd barely met Ellie, but already she knew in her gut she had someone to confide in. "Something really strange has happened. Can I talk to you in person?"

"Of course, dear. Would you like me to come to your house?" Ellie had grown increasingly confident at navigating her way around D.C. despite an entourage of reporters.

"I'll come to your hotel if that's okay. I'll be there in twenty minutes."

Ellie glowed with warmth as she opened the door, and Ariella felt oddly relaxed in her presence despite her dramatic news. This one person would know exactly how she felt.

Ellie ushered Ariella into the large suite that ANS had reserved for her, and they sat on the sofa. "What's going on? You look white as a sheet."

"I'm pregnant."

Ellie drew in a breath. "Oh, no."

Ariella's throat closed. This was not exactly the comforting response she'd been hoping for. Though she had to admit it was her own initial reaction. "It's okay. I'm perfectly healthy and I'm in a pretty okay financial situation to have a baby." Now she was trying to soothe her mother, not the other way around. The irony of the situation made her want to laugh.

"Do you love him?" Ellie's question shocked her.

"I don't know. We've only been seeing each other a few weeks. It's Simon, who you met in London."

"Oh, dear." Ellie's face crumpled.

Ariella put a hand on her arm. "What's the matter?"

"I feel like history's repeating itself. Why couldn't you be pregnant by a nice ordinary man who could marry you and live a comfortable ordinary life?"

"Simon's surprisingly ordinary for a prince." She tried to smile. "Okay, maybe not ordinary but he's very warm and down to earth."

"But his family. Those royals are absolutely bound by tradition. That's why Prince Charles couldn't marry Camilla in the first place like he should have."

"He's married to her now, isn't he?"

"Yes, but." She sighed. "So much sadness happened in the meantime. I'm still not sure they're ready to welcome an American into the family."

"Me, either, to be quite honest." She lifted her brows. "I socialized with them at a polo match last weekend and I felt like any of them would have happily driven me to the airport right then and there."

Ellie stroked her hand and looked softly into her eyes. "So they're not going to be too happy about you having his baby."

Ariella's breathing was steadily becoming shallower. She stopped and drew in a deep draught of air. She certainly didn't need her baby to be deprived of oxygen at this crucial stage in his or her development.

She laughed.

"What?" Ellie's eyes widened. She was probably wondering if Ariella had lost her mind.

"I was thinking about my baby. I wonder if it will be a boy or a girl."

Ellie's eyes brightened. "I always knew I was having a

girl. I dreamed of little girl dresses and dolls and all kinds of frilly pink things over and over again."

"And you were right." Though Ellie had never had a chance to enjoy dressing her daughter in fluffy dresses or buying her Barbie dolls with extravagant wardrobes.

Ellie's blue eyes suddenly shone with tears. "You won't give the baby up, will you?"

"Not a chance of it. I'm lucky that I've had a good career for a few years now and I have some savings. I can work right through the pregnancy, and probably hire a nanny soon afterward and work from home a lot. It's very doable." She was trying to convince herself as much as her mother.

Ellie smiled through her sudden tears. "You're much more confident and capable than I was. That's a blessing." Then her face grew serious. "Have you told Simon yet?"

Ariella shook her head. "I haven't told anyone yet. You're the first."

Ellie gasped, and suddenly their arms were around each other. "That's a great honor."

"An honor?" Ariella buried her face in her mother's soft hair. "You were the first person I thought of when I needed to tell someone. I can't even begin to tell you how happy I am to have you back in my life."

"Back in your life?" Ellie pulled back a little. "They took you from me as soon as you were born. They never even let me see you." Her eyes still glittered with tears. "They said it was for the best, but even then I knew they were wrong."

"You took care of me for the nine months that I was growing inside you. During that time we formed a bond that could never be broken. Not really."

Ellie breathed in slowly. "I thought about you every day for all of those twenty-eight years."

"See? In a strange way we were always connected, and you came back into my life just when I need you the most."

Her chest heaved as she held her mother tight. It was going to be okay. But first she had to tell Simon.

Simon couldn't stop whistling. It was midmorning and he'd been floating on air ever since he got off the plane in D.C. the previous evening. He had some urgent business to attend to and now Ariella was on the top of his agenda. She had invited him to her apartment, and he took that as a very promising sign. She'd been cool on the phone lately— when he could even reach her. Suddenly she wanted to see him, and as soon as possible. Apparently meeting his family hadn't scared her off as much as he thought.

The sweet and gracious way Ariella had handled his large and intimidating family further confirmed that she was the perfect woman for him. He'd trusted his instincts when he first saw her across that crowded ballroom, and so far they had been dead-on. She was *the one they talked about,* who came along once in a lifetime. He felt it deep in his gut. Or was it his heart? His whole body sang with emotions that he'd only read about in books before. He didn't plan to waste his once-in-a-lifetime chance at happiness. Now all he had to do was convince Ariella herself that they were meant to be together.

His jacket pocket bulged slightly with the tooled leather box delivered just before he left. Nestled in white satin was the loveliest ring he'd ever seen. He had to admit he hadn't paid too much attention to engagement rings before, but once he'd decided to propose, he did extensive research among his female friends.

He made up the elaborate excuse that he might be interested in helping promote the sale of African diamonds to help his charity, and he wanted some feedback on designs. He wasn't entirely sure they fell for it, but he got a lot of great information anyway: not too bulky; flashy is fine but not for everyone; steer clear of color unless you know it's one she adores. There was a long list he'd carried in his mind to the jeweler.

With the help—and promised discretion—of the queen's appointed jeweler, he'd chosen a stunning, very pale pink diamond with a provenance dating back to the maharajas of India. Together they'd designed a setting of tiny diamonds and, since she always wore silver jewelry rather than gold, a simple platinum setting. The jeweler's workshop had put the ring together almost overnight and he was convinced that it was the perfect ring for Ariella and that she'd adore it.

If she'd agree to be his wife.

He wasn't nearly so confident about that part. Ariella wasn't the type to accept just because he was a prince— which was one of the many reasons he loved her. He'd missed her so much since she'd returned to D.C. Playing it cool and not bombarding her with phone calls had been torture. He ached to see her again. To put his arms around her and kiss her as if the world was ending. He'd never felt even a fraction of this passion for a woman before. He knew his intense feelings meant that Ariella was the only woman for him.

The car pulled up in front of Ariella's tidy Georgetown house and he got out. A sizzle of anticipation ran through him as he saw the lights were on in her first-floor apartment. He intended to build up to the proposal. He'd woo her and get the mood romantic before he plunged in with the question of a lifetime.

She'd had cold feet the last time he saw her. He'd be sure to warm them up and reassure her that even the most intractable members of his family would come to their senses. The monarchy hadn't survived for so many years by being inflexible. No one was going to force him out of the country or make him give up his position in the royal family because of whom he loved. Together they'd slowly but surely win them over and make them realize that an infusion of fresh energy from across the Atlantic was just what they all needed. He'd kiss her until she was weak in the knees and maybe even make love to her until they lay spent in each other's arms—then he'd ask her.

His driver handed him the big bunch of pink roses he'd ordered. No doubt any nearby photographers would have a field day, but soon enough they'd all be scribbling the story of their engagement so it didn't really matter what they were speculating. In fact he welcomed them heralding the happy news that he and Ariella would spend the rest of their lives together.

He climbed the steps to her building with glowing anticipation and rang the bell a little too long. The first sight of her face after a two-week absence almost made him shout. She was unquestionably the most beautiful woman on earth, with her long dark hair tumbling about her shoulders and those big, soulful eyes fixed right on him.

When he flung his arms around her, still clutching the roses in one fist, he noticed she seemed a little stiff. "It's so good to see you again."

"Yes." Her answer seemed a little less than enthusiastic.

"I brought you some roses. I thought they might remind you of our English rose gardens."

She smiled. "Your country does have the most beautiful gardens in the world."

They were talking about gardens? He was dying to propose to her and get it over with, as the suspense was killing him. But something wasn't right. She looked pale. "How are you?"

She ushered him into the apartment. Wordless, her shoulders slightly hunched, she seemed very tense. "Please sit down."

He frowned. "I feel like you're about to drop some kind of bombshell. I'm not going to fall down like an old granny."

That gentle smile hovered about her mouth again. "I'm sure you wouldn't, but just in case."

"You do have a bombshell to drop?" His mind ran through the possibilities. Her father had asked her to go live in the White House and forbidden her from dating? She couldn't take the press anymore and had decided to go underground? Aliens had invaded and...

"I'm pregnant."

Ten

Ariella watched as Simon's amused expression faded to a blank. "What?"

"I know it's hard to believe, but I took a test and it was positive."

"We didn't have sex until...two weeks ago. Is that even long enough to know you're pregnant?" He stared at her in astonishment and confusion.

"Apparently so." Did he think she was pregnant by someone else and had decided to pin the blame on him in the hope of a big royal payoff? Indignation stirred in her chest. "Don't worry, I don't expect anything of you. I know the timing is terrible and it's the last thing we expected, but it's happened and I intend to raise the baby. I'm financially well off, so you don't need to worry that I'll ask for money."

"That's the last thing I'm worried about." He blinked, staring at her. "We used a condom."

Apparently he still didn't believe it was possible. "It could have leaked or broken or who knows what. They're not very effective. At this point it doesn't really matter. I'm definitely pregnant." She'd done another two tests. Different brands, same result.

"Wow." He climbed to his feet and came toward her. "Congratulations."

She laughed. "You don't have to congratulate me. We both know it was a big accident."

"Still, it feels like an occasion for celebration." He reached into his pocket and pulled something out.

Oh, no. A leather box. Her heart seized as she realized what he was about to do. Could she refuse a proposal before it was even made?

He got onto one knee, confirming her worst fears. "Ariella." His eyes were smiling, which seemed downright strange under the circumstances. "Will you marry me?"

She bit her lip, hoping to hold back sudden and pointless tears that threatened. She couldn't seem to get words out so she simply shook her head.

He frowned. "You won't? Why not?" His sudden indignation would be funny if she didn't feel so sad. This must be one more sign that they weren't meant to be. It didn't seem to cross his mind that she might have her own opinion and it could be different from his. Probably being a prince trained you to think that everyone was on your side and wholeheartedly agreed with you.

"It would never work." Her voice came out broken and raspy. "Your family would be horrified. They made it abundantly clear that they intend for you to marry someone else."

"They'll get over it." His gaze turned steely.

"No they won't. I've seen enough press coverage of your family to know they're very set in their ways. I don't want to be the outcast and black sheep for the rest of my life. Nor do I want the queen to take away your beloved estate or kick you out of your charity. You've built a life that you love and marrying me would ruin everything, so it's not going to happen."

The truth of her words echoed inside her. She truly didn't want those things to happen, for Simon or for herself.

"Why are you talking about everyone else? I want to marry *you*. Now that you're pregnant there's all the more reason to do it, and soon." He was still on one knee in front of the sofa where she sat. The whole situation seemed ridiculous. Especially as his words were undermining her conviction. Could they really just forget about his family and the reporters and the British public and her presidential father and do what they wanted?

No. They couldn't. Life didn't work like that.

He smacked his head suddenly. "In all this talk about a baby and my family, I think I forgot to mention the most important thing." He took hold of her hands. "Which is that I love you. I never knew what love was until I met you. Every minute I'm not with you I'm wishing I was. When I am with you I don't want to leave. I want to spend the rest of my life with you, Ariella. I need to spend the rest of my life with you. I love you."

Her chest tightened as he tried to put such strong feelings into mere words and those words rocked her to her core. What hurt most was that she felt the same way. Since Simon came into her life nothing else seemed very important any more. But the truth was that the world was still out there, and hoping and dreaming wasn't enough to build a life on. "Love doesn't last forever. It's a brief flash of excitement and enthusiasm that brings people together. The rest of it is work. I know my parents—the ones who raised me—worked hard to keep their marriage strong in the face of all the tiresome details of life. My birth parents obviously couldn't manage to do that."

She frowned and stood up. She needed to put a little distance between them so she could think straight. It was hard to even speak with his big, masculine presence looming over her and his rich scent tugging at her senses. "There's a fierce attraction between us." She walked away from him, with her back turned. It was easier to speak when she couldn't see his bold, chiseled features. "It takes hold of me and makes me forget about everything else when I'm with you." Then she turned to face him. He'd risen to his feet and seemed to fill the space of her living room. "But that will fade. You were born with your whole life planned out for you. You're already married to your family and your country. You can't abandon them to marry someone who they disapprove of and who will never fit in. It was disastrous for your ancestor Edward VII and it would be disastrous for you." Tears fell down her cheeks and she couldn't stop them. "It's better for all of us if we break it off right now."

Simon exhaled loudly, like he'd been bottling up words and emotions inside him. "You're right. I am married to my family and my country and I'd never give them up. I know it's a lot to ask of you to embrace those things and love them as I do, but I am asking that." He strode toward her and took her hands. She wanted to pull away and attempt to keep some distance and objectivity, but he held them softly, but firmly, and she wasn't able to break free. "Marry me, Ariella."

Her gut churned. Her nerve endings cracked with an effusive "Yes!" but her brain issued loud warning signals. "I don't want you to marry me out of a sense of duty, because I'm pregnant."

"I'm not asking you because you're pregnant." Amusement sparkled in his eyes. "I bought the ring before I knew about the pregnancy. I was planning to build up to my proposal and do some romantic beating about the bush before springing the big question on you, but your surprise announcement made that seem superfluous. I want to marry you, pregnant or not, Ariella Winthrop, and I'm not leaving until you say yes."

"You're planning to bully me into it?" She stiffened. Sometimes his boundless enthusiasm and confidence were appealing, and sometimes it was a little scary.

He softened his grip on her hand. "No." He spoke softly. "There I go, running roughshod again. I apologize. I truly wish to embrace a lifetime of your moderating influence on my overly ebullient personality."

He said it so sweetly that her heart squeezed. She did believe him. "I don't think anyone could squash your bubble too much." She chuckled. It touched her deeply that he'd congratulated her on carrying their baby. For the first time it occurred to her that maybe he wanted to be congratulated, too. "I'm sure you're going to be a wonderful father, even if we aren't married."

"That's true, I will be." He hesitated. She could almost feel him bursting to insist that they would be married, but holding himself back, trying not to offend her.

"You're a wonderful man, Simon. I'm totally overwhelmed right now with all the publicity about my father, and my mother and the TV special. It's almost ridiculous that I met you at the same time. It would be crazy to leap into an unplanned marriage without thinking long and hard about the consequences. Perhaps at some time in the future we can discuss it again and…who knows?" She trailed off, running out of words. Part of her wanted to run screaming away from Simon and everyone else and hide from reality.

The rest of her wanted to rush to him and throw herself into his strong arms and let him take care of her the way he so confidently intended to.

"I'm not leaving, if that's what you were trying to hint at." That familiar gleam of humor shone in his eyes. "Me and my ring will sit quietly in the corner until you come to your senses."

"As if that was possible." She couldn't help smiling. "I doubt you could sit quietly anywhere for more than about three minutes."

"Three whole minutes?" He rubbed his mouth thoughtfully. "You could be right. In the meantime, you should be eating for two so I think we need to go out for a hearty lunch."

She laughed. "You're impossible."

"I'm all about making the impossible possible. They said I couldn't raft up the Zambezi or ascend the north face of Mount Everest. They laughed when I talked about internet access in the Masai Mara. I proved them all wrong. If they say an American isn't a suitable bride for a British prince, then I'll spend the rest of my life proving them wrong about that as well, and have fun doing it."

His passion made her heart swell. But he was talking as if she was just another mountain to climb. "You do make a compelling case for your own convictions, but you don't seem to be listening to me."

"How?" His look of confusion made her want to laugh again.

"I said I'm not ready to commit to anything right now. I've had the biggest shocks of my life these past few months and I barely know which end is up."

His expression grew serious. "Point taken. I'll stop pushing my agenda. Now, how about that lunch?"

"That, I'll agree to." And she let him take her hand and

help her up from the sofa. His skin sparked arousal as it touched hers. She hid a silent sigh from him. Why did her life have to be so complicated?

She frowned when Simon's driver pulled up in front of Talesin. The navy awnings created cool shade in front of one of the most exclusive restaurants in D.C. Unease trickled through her. "Are we eating here?"

"Their steaks are world famous. You need iron rich foods."

"Why does everything you say make me laugh?" Then she glanced about. "Did you know it's the president's favorite restaurant?" What if they ran into him here? She hadn't seen him since the dinner they'd shared after the taping, though he'd sent her several warm emails and they were talking about a weekend together at Camp David, the presidential retreat in Maryland.

"Is it really?" He helped her out of the car. "I've been meaning to eat here for ages."

"It's probably hard to get a table without a reservation." She remembered one tense afternoon of scrambling to book a room for an important client's dinner there.

He leaned in and whispered. "Not when you're a prince."

She chuckled. "Oh yes, I forgot about that."

"Welcome to Talesin, Your Highness." The imperious maître d' nodded and gestured warmly. "A table for two?"

"Thank you." Simon shot her an amused smile. "See what I mean?"

She arched a brow. "Don't get cocky."

"I'll do my best."

The maître d' led them through the main dining room and out onto a shady patio with a view over the river.

"Ariella." The now-familiar voice made her turn to find the president standing behind her.

"Oh, hello. How nice to see you." She felt a surge of panic. "Simon, this is President Morrow, my…my father. And this is Simon Worth." Should she have used the word *prince?* She hadn't researched the correct way to address him. Luckily, being Simon, he wasn't likely to mind.

Ted Morrow smiled at Simon. "Would you both do me the honor of joining me in my private dining room?"

"I… We…" She glanced at Simon.

"I suspect we'd be delighted." Simon glanced at her, a question in his eyes.

"Yes. Yes, we would." She swallowed. Simon *and* her father, the president? An odd nagging feeling suggested that this was a little too much of a coincidence.

They followed the president back inside the building through a doorway that led into a bright room with tall windows and elegant furnishings that were a mix of eighteenth century and modernist Italian design. The professional side of her brain wondered if it could be rented out for special occasions, while the personal side of her brain wondered what the heck they would talk about.

The restaurant's most trusted staff waited on them hand and foot, recommending dishes and bringing bottles of wine. She learned that the president had a policy of only drinking American wine, and it made her like him more, considering the other options that must be available in the White House cellars alone. She managed to refuse the wine by saying she didn't drink during the day, but the moment did serve as a reminder that there was a fourth person in the room—her unborn child. And Simon's unborn child. Ted Morrow's grandchild. Her whole life seemed like an elaborate spider web that kept expanding to encompass more of the people around her.

Simon kept the conversation going with easy banter about traveling and the parts of America that he hadn't seen yet but wanted to. Ariella was constantly amazed by how naturally he could talk to anyone. No doubt it was the chief requirement of his role in the royal family and if she were his boss she'd give him a raise. She'd actually started to relax by the time they finished their delicious appetizers and three gleaming steaks arrived, accompanied by mounds of fresh vegetables. Even her shaky pregnancy appetite felt revived by the sight.

"This is turning out to be the most extraordinary year of my life by quite a long way," said her father, after a pause while they all chewed their meals. "I thought last year with the run-up to the elections would be hard to beat, but it has been, and hands down. And the best thing of all has been learning that I have a beautiful daughter."

He gazed at her with such warmth that she felt emotion swell in her chest. "It does seem like a wonderful thing now that the media frenzy is dying down and we can finally get to know each other."

"And if the press hadn't found you, I might never have seen Ellie again. I had no idea she'd moved to Ireland, and if it wasn't for this whole brouhaha, she might never have come back to the States."

"I think she's considering moving back here for good."

He smiled. "I know. And she told me that the two of you are becoming close."

Ariella blanched. Ellie hadn't told him the secret of her pregnancy, had she? No. She knew her mother would never do that. She'd kept her own secrets for so long she could be trusted. Suddenly she hated herself for the subterfuge, but she knew it was too soon to tell anyone. At least until she and Simon had a few things figured out. "We are just getting to know each other but already she's becoming one of my favorite people on earth. I'm trying to convince her to stay in the D.C. area for now, so she we can all try to make up for lost time."

The president paused and took a sip of his white wine. "Making up for lost time is something that's been on my mind a lot." He put down his glass. "I loved your mother with all my heart, Ariella. I would never have let her go. She just didn't know that at the time. I was being a typical man and bottling up my emotions, trying to act cool."

Ariella glanced at Simon. He wouldn't do that. He was the last person to keep anything bottled up. It was one of the things she liked best about him. There were no guessing games with him. "Have you told her how you felt?"

"You'd better believe it." He smiled wistfully. "It was the first thing I did when we had a few moments alone. I apologized with all my heart for the fact that she felt so alone back then, and was forced into a choice she later regretted." He frowned and looked down at his glass, then looked up at her again. "I still love her, you know."

Ariella's eyes widened. She was mostly astonished that he was saying all this in front of Simon, who—as far as she knew—he'd only just met. "Have you told her that?"

"I most certainly have. I think she was astonished rather than delighted." He smiled. "We've been spending a lot of time together."

"That's wonderful." Her heart filled with gladness at the thought that her mother and father could rekindle their love after all these years. What a shame that they'd had twenty-eight years apart. "Is she the reason you never married?"

He nodded. "I tried to talk myself into loving other women, but when it came to the crunch none of them compared to my Ellie and I could never marry a woman I didn't feel wholeheartedly committed to."

"That's my opinion entirely." Simon chimed in. "I think

that choosing your mate is the most important decision you'll make in your entire life."

"Quite right, son. It's not a decision to be taken lightly." Her father looked at Ariella with a twinkle of amusement in his eye. "Which is what I told this young man when he demanded an audience with me to request your hand in marriage."

Ariella's jaw dropped. So they had met before. And this meeting was preplanned. Simon had been sneaking around behind her back. Indignation snapped inside her and she turned to Simon. "What were you thinking?"

"In our country, it's traditional to ask the father of an intended bride if he objects to the marriage. Given the sensitive circumstances of your father's position, I felt I should listen to any objections he might have."

The president laughed. "And you'd better believe I had them." He reached out and took Ariella's hand across the table. "I told him he'd better direct any important questions of that nature to the lady intended, not to me. Since I've been in your life for less than two weeks I don't feel I should have any say whatsoever over who you marry or don't marry." He squeezed her hand. "He's got a lot of chutzpah, I'll say that for him."

Simon smiled. "He told me to stop beating about the bush and go ask you. Which I did. So now I've asked both of you."

"Oh." Ariella's heart clenched as she realized the president was waiting to hear what answer she'd given Simon.

Ted Morrow looked at Simon. "Could I have a few moments alone with my daughter?"

"Certainly, sir." Simon rose from the table. He'd already finished his meal while they were talking. He smiled at Ariella. "I'll be on the balcony."

The door closed behind him, and Ariella frowned.

Should she tell her father she'd said no to him? Should she confess the truth about her pregnancy? It was all too much and her tired and emotional brain couldn't handle it.

"Well, isn't that something. I'm a guy from a small town in Montana and I just told a member of the British royal family to leave the room."

"And I'm a girl from a small town in Montana and I'm having lunch with the president of the United States."

He nodded and smiled, and his blue eyes sparkled. "I guess it proves we're all just people once you look past the pomp and circumstance." His expression grew serious. "Do you love him?"

She twisted her water glass in her hands. "I think I might."

"You don't sound too sure."

"We really…click. I guess that's the best way to put it. I have so much fun with him and I always feel relaxed in his company, which is really weird under the circumstances." She did not feel the need to mention the intense sexual attraction. "I like him very, very much. But the fact is, we only met a few weeks ago and they've been some of the craziest weeks of my life and I don't know what to think about anything anymore."

"Well, I'll give you a piece of advice that might be worth exactly what it'll cost you." He inhaled. "Don't wait around for the 'right time' when everything falls into place and feels perfect." He fixed his eyes on hers. "In my experience, which is considerable at this point, that time never comes."

She nodded slowly.

He leaned forward and took her hand again. His hands were big and warm and soft. "If you love this young man— and from what I see in your eyes, I think you do—don't blow the love of a lifetime because it doesn't fit your calendar. I went off to college naively assuming that Ellie and the whole life I had planned out with her would still be there when I got back." He shook his head. "Instead I got back to find that she'd left town and no one knew where she was. My entire future evaporated overnight just like that. Sure, I got the college education I wanted and then started the big career I'd always hoped for, but the soul of my life, the really important part, had got on a train one dark night and skipped town without me."

His eyes were now soft with tears. "I missed Ellie so much those first few years. Then I suppose I grew numb, or grew used to the dull ache of living without her. When I think of the memories we could have shared it infuriates me that I missed out on all that through my own stupid fault. I should have married her and taken her to college with me instead of stupidly insisting on waiting until the time was right. Yes, times would have been hard and we would have had to scrimp a bit, but we would have had each other, and that's the important thing. If you love this young man, then don't miss out on the opportunity of a lifetime." He squeezed her hand softly. "I don't want you to live to regret it like I did."

Ariella's chest was so tight she could hardly breathe. "I'm having his baby. I just found out this week." She had no idea how he'd react, but she knew she couldn't keep it to herself any longer.

His mouth made a funny movement, like he wanted to say something but was too choked up.

"I told Ellie a couple of days ago and she urged me not to hide it from Simon. I took her advice today. It almost feels like history is repeating itself, doesn't it?"

Her father shook his head. "No, Ariella. History isn't repeating itself because you and Simon are braver and stronger and maybe a little more bullheaded than Ellie and I were." He laughed. "Simon's quite a young man. I don't think you could go far wrong with him in your life."

She smiled. "I know. He's pretty amazing." Then she swallowed. "But then there's the rest of his family. And we'd have to live in England."

He shrugged. "England's just across the pond. A short plane flight. Simon told me he'd already introduced you to the whole family."

"Did he also tell you they were all trying to pack my bags and get me on the next flight back to D.C.?"

Ted frowned. "He didn't mention that part."

"He glosses over it like it's no big deal. He thinks they'd all come around. I'm not so sure."

"Well, I'm inclined to agree with Simon since he knows them better than you. And it probably doesn't hurt that your father is commander in chief of their largest ally." He winked.

She smiled, but then her stomach lurched as she remembered his uncle's cruel threats. "His uncle Derek warned me Simon could lose his estate and his charity if he doesn't follow the party line."

Ted laughed. "I wouldn't worry about that old coot. He has bigger problems to worry about than an American in the family. The CIA chief just informed me that he was involved in brokering an arms deal with a South American dictatorship."

"What?"

"Yup. I don't think he'll be hassling you too much after that scandal explodes in the press."

Ariella stared, speechless.

"Greed. That's what made him do it. Apparently he doesn't have the income of the rest of the bunch but he's trying to live like an emperor. The insecure ones are usually the meanest. That's what I've noticed."

"You've made me feel a lot better." She did feel like a weight had lifted. The queen had been stern, but not actually hostile. Derek was the only one who'd told her to get lost in no uncertain terms. And now he was going to be public enemy number one himself. She couldn't help smiling. "I think I can handle Uncle Derek."

"I suspect you can handle a lot more than one narrow-minded Limey, though I suppose I should stop calling them that if there's going to be one in the family. Shall we invite him back in for dessert?"

"Yes." She grinned. "Let's do that."

Ted opened the door to the balcony and called Simon back. He arrived with another woman on his arm—her mother.

Ariella gasped. "What kind of conspiracy is this?"

Ted Morrow kissed Ellie on both cheeks. "I asked Ellie to join us for coffee because I can't stand to be away from her for more than a few minutes."

Her mother was transformed from the pale and harried woman she'd first met in London. A soft jade-green dress hugged her girlish figure, and the light of passion shone in her green eyes. "And I feel the same way. It's embarrassing for someone my age." She blushed sweetly. Ted Morrow took her hand and led her to a chair right next to his. He seemed besotted with her. Ariella watched in astonishment.

"Did your father tell you how annoyed he was with me seeking his opinion before I asked for yours?" Simon slid his arm around her waist.

"Not really." Heat rose through her as she felt his body through their clothing. "He told me not to blow what might be the love of a lifetime."

"Excellent advice," Simon murmured. His breath stirred

the tiny hairs on her neck and sent shivers of desire running through her. "I hope you listened."

"I did. Did someone mention dessert?" She pulled away from him and reached for the hand-written dessert menu. It felt embarrassing to be romantic in front of her parents.

Though come to think of it, they were getting rather romantic themselves. Ted held Ellie's hands in his and they gazed into each other's eyes as if the rest of the world didn't exist.

"No, I don't believe anyone did mention dessert, but we don't want you starving, so let's get the trolley brought in." He smiled and looked at her belly.

Ariella's eyes widened. Then she realized that everyone in the room knew her secret, so it wasn't really a secret. "I am rather starving right now. Maybe there is something to the old wives' tales."

"Did you tell your dad whether you intend to marry me?"

"I did not." Ariella scanned the menu. Then she looked up, trying to keep her expression neutral while her heart swelled with emotion. "Though I'm pretty close to making up my mind."

"Torture is banned by the United Nations." Simon's imploring gaze made her want to laugh and touched her deeply at the same time.

She glanced at her parents, then tugged her eyes away quickly as they kissed each other softly on the lips, eyes closed in a rapture of togetherness. They'd lost twenty-eight years of happiness together, because they weren't ready to commit all those years ago. Because the timing wasn't right, they almost lost everything.

She drew in a long, slow breath, as conviction filled her heart, mind and lungs. "Yes, Simon Worth, I will marry you."

Epilogue

Three months later

Ariella woke up to the familiar sight of Simon's handsome face next to hers on the pillow in their shared bedroom in Whist Castle. He had scoffed at the notion that they should pretend to live apart until the wedding, and somehow the British public thought his honesty and disdain for tired etiquette was part of his charm. She'd been sharing his bed for a solid month now, since she'd finally packed up her D.C. apartment and her life in the States.

They hadn't told anyone about the baby yet. Somehow it made sense to keep the secret until after the ceremony, so the wedding preparations had to be rushed. She still wasn't showing, at least not in a way she couldn't pass off as the aftereffects of a large meal.

Their bodies were pressed together almost from chin to ankle. Somehow she always wound up on his side of the bed in the morning. It would be embarrassing if he didn't clearly enjoy it so much.

"Morning, gorgeous." Simon's husky voice sent a shiver of awareness through her.

"Same to you." Helicopters buzzed outside the windows, sending adrenaline streaking through her veins. "Is it really our wedding day or is this just a long, fantastical dream?"

"I'm not sure." He smiled, still resting on the pillow. "What do you think?"

She pretended to pinch herself. "I'm lying in a luxurious bed in a castle and getting ready to marry a prince. Sounds like a dream to me."

Simon leaned forward and planted a soft kiss on her lips. "How does that feel?" he murmured.

"Mmm. That feels real." Passion and warmth swelled in her chest and she slid her arms around him under the covers. "Breathtakingly real. But wait. You're not supposed to see me on my wedding day!" She pulled back, suddenly panicked. What else would she do wrong today?

Simon pulled her closer again. "There are some traditions best left by the wayside." He nuzzled her neck, which made her smile. "I'm probably not supposed to make love to you on the morning of your wedding, but luckily I have a rebellious streak."

"We can't. Can we?" Arousal trickled through her like music. "We have to get ready." She said it more as a question than a statement.

"We'll be ready when we need to. You're not planning this one, thank goodness."

She'd turned the reins of the wedding over to Scarlet and her new partner, and they'd done a spectacular job pulling together what promised to be the wedding of the century in less than three months. "It's hard for me not to worry about the details, though. What if the caterer can't get through the crowds to deliver the food?"

"Someone else's problem." He kissed her lips again.

Relaxation soaked through her veins. "You're very good at distracting me." She kissed him back, letting herself sink into his arms. Nothing ruffled Simon's feathers, at least not for long. He was so confident and capable that it was hard to be anxious around him.

His hands roamed over her chest, sparking trails of excitement, and she could feel his arousal thickening against her. "Uh-oh, are we really going to do this?"

"It's starting to look inevitable," he rasped.

"But we have a thousand guests coming. And our friends staying here at Whist are probably downstairs having breakfast right now."

"We'll see them soon enough."

He squeezed her backside, and she responded by pinching his gently, with a giggle. "You're a bad influence."

"I love you." He said it simply, and the truth of it punched her in the gut.

"I love you, too. I think I knew it from the first night I met you, which doesn't make any sense at all."

"Love isn't supposed to make sense." He smiled, looking into her eyes. "That's why it's so wonderful."

Her heart filled to overflowing. "If you weren't the most persistent and persuasive man on earth, I might never have dared to let myself fall in love with you."

"Tenacity has its virtues." He nibbled her earlobe, which made her gasp, then laugh. "Thank goodness I had your parents to help convince you to take a chance on me."

"And now they're getting married, too." She grinned, thinking about the rapturous looks Ellie and Ted always had on their faces when they were together. A president had never married while in office before, and the event, planned for a month's time, was to be the American equivalent of a royal wedding. She couldn't wait to be there and watch them finally pledge their vows to each other after so many wasted years.

A long steamy kiss sent blood racing through her veins and arousal trickling to her fingers and toes, and other parts.

"Come here, madam." Simon climbed over her, and slid his fingers over her hot, ready sex.

"Yes, Your Majesty." Her back was already arching, ready to receive him. Her fingers pushed into his thick hair as he entered her, making her gasp with pleasure. Wedding anxieties shriveled and floated up to the sky like embers as they moved together under the soft covers, reveling in each others' bodies. The sweet relief of their climax left them relaxed and ready to face anything.

"I can't believe we get to do this whenever we want for the rest of our lives," breathed Simon heavily, as they lay spent, with their heads on the same pillow again. "I'm the luckiest man on earth."

"We are lucky, aren't we? This year started out with all the shocking press revelations that I was the president's daughter, and spiraled out of control from there. I seem to have landed in a very soft place."

"Are you trying to say my body is soft?" He poked her gently.

"No one could accuse you of being soft. Well, except your heart."

"Okay, that I'll admit to. I'm just glad I found the right woman to give it to."

A knock on the door made them jump. "Sorry to disturb you," called a tentative voice. "But the dressmaker requires your presence for an urgent fitting."

"Oh, dear," she whispered. "I think we'd better get up."

"If we must." He nuzzled her face. "The best part is that tonight we'll be right back here together."

The ceremony took place in the estate's thirteenth-century chapel. Since the chapel was only large enough to seat immediate family, Simon and Ariella's vows were simultaneously broadcast to the gathered crowd of guests on the estate lawns and an eager viewing audience on both sides of the Atlantic. When they were declared man and wife, the newest royal couple joined the guests outside on a glorious summer's day.

Scarlet had planned and executed the wedding with skill and courage worthy of a major battle. Tables and chairs were arrayed across the rolling lawns, each decorated with fresh flowers, and, in a green touch that Ariella especially loved, an assortment of beautiful tableware and linens borrowed and bought from collections, antique stores and markets, for a spontaneous yet luxurious, country garden picnic feel.

Given the estate's large size and the volume of the crowd, they decided that one band wasn't enough, so in addition to the traditional orchestra, they had an African ensemble, a bluegrass band and a group of singers from the Westminster Abbey boys' choir, who wandered the grounds serenading guests as they mingled on the lawns and nibbled delicacies at their tables.

Ariella saw Scarlet rearranging a Meissen jug full of roses, and hurried over to her. "Hey, lady, you're not supposed to be working today. You're here as a guest, remember?"

Scarlet spun around, red curls flying. "Old habits die hard, though the team we hired is doing a great job. I'm surprised you're not rearranging the glasses yourself."

"It's taking a lot of discipline." She grinned. "But I'm working hard to retrain myself."

"I'm still ticked off that you're leaving DC Affairs. You could have been our British office."

"I'll have my hands full arranging events for the palace."

"Lucky you." Scarlet sighed. "The most magnificent venues in England at your fingertips. And the most sought-after guests as your family. How did the queen feel about Simon choosing you as his bride?"

"I was very nervous about it but weirdly enough she was lovely to me from the first moment Simon told her he'd proposed to me. She said she could see how perfect I was for him and she welcomed me into the family. Probably the biggest surprise of my life. And with her on my side everyone else welcomed me, too. Simon's brothers are so sweet—it's like having brothers of my own."

"How did you talk them into letting you plan their parties?"

"I could see they needed someone with an imagination to take over. They were still throwing the same parties that seemed fun during post-war rationing. I told them I can provide ten times the flair for half the money, so they're letting me go wild. British people really know how to party when they get a chance."

"So I've noticed." Scarlet glanced around with a grin.

"And some of the Americans are getting crazy, too. I saw you and Daniel dancing like demons to the bluegrass a while ago."

"Daniel's definitely mined my fun-loving streak. Before, I always enjoyed watching other people have fun at events. Now I'm realizing how great it is to be one of them." She glanced up. "Cara's just as bad as me. She's only supposed to be managing PR for the event, but look, she's trying to retie the bow on that table skirt even though she's so pregnant she can barely bend." They hurried over to her. "Drop that bow or we'll send you on enforced maternity leave."

Cara had recently left the White House press office after she fell in love with a network news reporter, and now worked with DC Affairs. She had that famous maternal glow already, her eyes shining and her chestnut hair glowing. "I have more than a month left before I'm due. You should indulge me now as I may not be capable of anything once I'm only getting two hours of sleep a night."

Cara's husband, Max, appeared, glass of champagne in hand. "Max, darling." Ariella kissed his cheek. "You need to rein your wife in. She's trying to do everything again."

"I've talked to her about that and she's still unstoppable. She should never have agreed to work with DC Affairs. You and Scarlet are a bad influence."

"It must be killing you that ANS is getting the scoop on the wedding." Ariella and Simon had decided that ANS should have exclusive coverage of the wedding as a reward for Liam skillfully orchestrating her reunion with her parents. Until recently Max had been the popular anchor of a rival TV network and still worked for them behind the scenes.

"I'm over it. It's a nice change to be able to enjoy a royal wedding instead of barking about it while standing on a street corner somewhere. I notice Liam's busy dancing with Francsesca. Isn't he supposed to be manning the scoop of the century?"

"Nope." Ariella crossed her arms. "None of my friends is allowed to work today, by royal command. Anyone caught working will be thrown into a dungeon."

Max glanced up at the ivy-covered walls of Whist Castle. "Hmm, that sounds like an interesting experience. Maybe I could do a live feed—"

"Oh, stop." Ariella laughed. "Have you seen my husband? We've only been married forty minutes and I've already lost him."

Scarlet nodded toward the area near the champagne bar. "He's locked in conversation with my husband. I think Simon's trying to convince Daniel to expand his network into Africa." Daniel owned a social networking site that had helped spread the word about the concert for World Connect. "I still can't believe you guys managed to get Pitbull, Beyoncé and Jay-Z and Eric Clapton all on the same stage, and only two weeks before your wedding, no less."

"Uh, hello, don't forget Mick Jagger and Aretha Franklin." Ariella still glowed with pleasure at how incredible a success the concert had been.

"Seriously, you guys are a force to be reckoned with."

"The concert was for an awesome cause so it was easy to get people excited." She smiled. "I'm going to Africa with Simon next month to raise awareness of his projects there."

"Look out, Africa." Max grinned. "There's no question that you and Simon are the most popular couple in the whole world. I didn't think his older brother's romance could be outshone but you've proved me wrong."

"At least they don't seem to hate me." Ariella shrugged. "I wasn't at all sure how the British people would react. I can truly say they've welcomed me with open arms. Not that they had much choice with Simon around." From where they stood she could see the queen in apparently intent conversation with her father.

"How could the British people not love you?" Lucy had strolled up with her husband Hayden and his curious toddler. She was a former reporter for ANS where she and Hayden had discovered that her own stepfather, then head of the network, had approved the illegal phone tapping that had revealed Ariella's parentage. Lucy became friends with Scarlet and Ariella after hiring DC Affairs to arrange her own wedding. "I know Liam takes full credit for reuniting you with your dad, and for getting Ted and Eleanor back together."

"All of our ears are burning." Ted Morrow walked up behind Ariella with Eleanor on his arm. He looked both statesmanlike and warm at the same time, and Ellie looked radiant in a stunning Narciso Rodriguez dress Ariella had helped her choose.

Liam was hot on his heels. "I'm shamelessly trying to negotiate exclusive coverage of your father and mother's wedding. A president hasn't married in office since 1915."

Ted Morrow beamed. "I told this nice young man that I'm far too busy enjoying my daughter's wedding to think about my own just yet." He turned and kissed Ellie softly on the cheek. "Though we freely admit that it will happen this year." A big fat rock sparkled on Ellie's slim hand. "We have a few other things to do first. After this shindig winds down we're heading to Ireland to visit the village where my beautiful Ellie was hidden away for so long."

"They'll be really happy to meet Ted." Ellie gazed at him adoringly. "After my husband died five years ago, people started pestering me to date again, and I never wanted to. I seem to have changed my mind."

"Thanks to my efforts, of course." Liam beamed. "Everyone told me you'd never come on air for the reunion, even Ariella. But I've never been one to take no for an answer. If I had I wouldn't have won my own bride." He squeezed Francesca, who grinned. She wore a stunning ruched dress that made her look like an Italian bombshell. "She would have told me the stars weren't aligned right, or something. Speaking of stars, here comes Prince Charming."

Simon walked over and waved. "You all know my cousin Colin, right?" He gestured to the tall blond man walking next to him. "He's the diplomat who negotiated the privacy rights treaty that brought me to the U.S. in the first place."

"Where I found my wife, Rowena." Colin squeezed the pretty woman at his side.

Rowena waved hello. "I'm having the time of my life here in Colin's home country. Everyone's so sweet." She held the hand of her toddler son. Ariella had made sure that all children of the guests were invited as well. Who would want to go away for a weekend to a foreign country without their children?

"Ah, we're not always that sweet." Simon kissed Ariella on the cheek. "My wife can tell you that sometimes we're as stubborn as mules."

"I like to think of that as part of our charm." Colin smiled. "It certainly can be an advantage in foreign diplomacy."

They all laughed. Simon raised his glass. "I hope you'll all be regular guests here at Whist Castle. We intend to travel back to the States as often as possible so it's only fair that you all return the favor."

Ted Morrow lifted his glass. "I'll drink to that. As long as you don't start trying to tax our tea, we'll get along just fine."

"You Americans barely even drink tea," Simon protested. "One time I ordered tea in a D.C. restaurant and they brought me an ice cold glass of dishwater with a slice of lemon in it. Very uncivilized."

Ted chuckled. "We'll be sure to have some of that dark

witches' brew you British enjoy on hand when you and Ariella come to stay at the White House."

"Don't forget the biscuits," Simon teased. "And they're not the big puffy ones dripping with butter that you Americans eat, either."

"I know." Ted smiled. "They're what we call cookies. Since my beloved Ellie has now lived on both sides of the Atlantic, she's helping me navigate the language barrier. It's wonderful being part of a big, international family."

Ariella beamed with pride as her handsome husband wrapped his strong arm around her waist. In a few short months she'd gone from being a lonely orphan to finding herself at the center of a large and growing family, with two loving parents, a sexy and adorable husband and a network of friends stretching around the world. Could anyone be luckier?

"Three cheers for Their Royal Highness," chimed in Colin. They all lifted their glasses. "Hip, hip!" called Colin, and the crowd roared a deafening, "Hooray!"

Ariella laughed. It would take her a while to get used the sometimes antiquated customs in her newly adopted homeland.

"Hip, hip!" yelled Colin.

"Hooray!" roared the guests.

But she'd have fun doing it, and sharing her life with the most caring and loving man she'd ever met.

"Hip, hip!"

The cheers had spread through the crowd and the final "Hooray" boomed across the lawns like rolling thunder.

* * * * *

REQUEST YOUR FREE BOOKS!
2 FREE NOVELS PLUS 2 FREE GIFTS!

◆ HARLEQUIN®

Desire

ALWAYS POWERFUL, PASSIONATE AND PROVOCATIVE

YES! Please send me 2 FREE Harlequin Desire® novels and my 2 FREE gifts (gifts are worth about $10). After receiving them, if I don't wish to receive any more books, I can return the shipping statement marked "cancel." If I don't cancel, I will receive 6 brand-new novels every month and be billed just $4.55 per book in the U.S. or $4.99 per book in Canada. That's a savings of at least 13% off the cover price! It's quite a bargain! Shipping and handling is just 50¢ per book in the U.S. and 75¢ per book in Canada.* I understand that accepting the 2 free books and gifts places me under no obligation to buy anything. I can always return a shipment and cancel at any time. Even if I never buy another book, the two free books and gifts are mine to keep forever.

225/326 HDN F4ZC

Name	(PLEASE PRINT)

Address		Apt. #

City	State/Prov.	Zip/Postal Code

Signature (if under 18, a parent or guardian must sign)

Mail to the Harlequin® Reader Service:
IN U.S.A.: P.O. Box 1867, Buffalo, NY 14240-1867
IN CANADA: P.O. Box 609, Fort Erie, Ontario L2A 5X3

**Want to try two free books from another line?
Call 1-800-873-8635 or visit www.ReaderService.com.**

* Terms and prices subject to change without notice. Prices do not include applicable taxes. Sales tax applicable in N.Y. Canadian residents will be charged applicable taxes. Offer not valid in Quebec. This offer is limited to one order per household. Not valid for current subscribers to Harlequin Desire books. All orders subject to credit approval. Credit or debit balances in a customer's account(s) may be offset by any other outstanding balance owed by or to the customer. Please allow 4 to 6 weeks for delivery. Offer available while quantities last.

Your Privacy—The Harlequin® Reader Service is committed to protecting your privacy. Our Privacy Policy is available online at www.ReaderService.com or upon request from the Harlequin Reader Service.

We make a portion of our mailing list available to reputable third parties that offer products we believe may interest you. If you prefer that we not exchange your name with third parties, or if you wish to clarify or modify your communication preferences, please visit us at www.ReaderService.com/consumerschoice or write to us at Harlequin Reader Service Preference Service, P.O. Box 9062, Buffalo, NY 14269. Include your complete name and address.

HD13R

SPECIAL EXCERPT FROM

HARLEQUIN®

Desire

USA TODAY *bestselling author*

Kathie DeNosky presents

A BABY BETWEEN FRIENDS, *part of the series*

THE GOOD, THE BAD AND THE TEXAN.

Available July 2013 from Harlequin® Desire®!

They fell into a comfortable silence while Ryder drove through the star-studded Texas night.

Her best friend was the real deal—honest, intelligent, easygoing and loyal to a fault. And it was only recently that she'd allowed herself to notice how incredibly good-looking he was. That was one reason she'd purposely waited until they were alone in his truck where it was dark so she wouldn't have to meet his gaze.

The time had come to start the conversation that would either help her dream come true—or send her in search of someone else to assist her.

"I've been doing a lot of thinking lately…" she began. "I miss being part of a family."

"I know, darlin'." He reached across the console to cover her hand with his. "But one day you'll find someone and settle down, and then you'll not only be part of his family, you can start one of your own."

"That's not going to happen," she said, shaking her head. "I have absolutely no interest in getting married. These days it's quite common for a woman to choose single motherhood."

"Well, there are a lot of kids who need a good home," he concurred, his tone filled with understanding.

"I'm not talking about adopting," Summer said, "at least not yet. I'd like to experience all aspects of motherhood, if I can, and that includes being pregnant."

"The last I heard, being pregnant is kind of difficult without the benefit of a man being involved," he said with a wry smile.

"Yes, to a certain degree, a man would need to be involved."

"Oh, so you're going to visit a sperm bank?" He didn't sound judgmental and she took that as a positive sign.

"No." She shook her head. "I'd rather know my baby's father."

Ryder looked confused. "Then how do you figure on making this happen if you're unwilling to wait until you meet someone and you don't want to visit a sperm bank?"

Her pulse sped up. "I have a donor in mind."

"Well, I guess if the guy's agreeable that would work," he said thoughtfully. "Anybody I know?"

"Yes." She paused for a moment to shore up her courage. Then, before she lost her nerve, she blurted out, "I want you to be the father of my baby, Ryder."

Will Ryder say yes?

Find out in Kathie DeNosky's new novel

A BABY BETWEEN FRIENDS

Available July 2013 from Harlequin® Desire®!

ALWAYS POWERFUL, PASSIONATE AND PROVOCATIVE.

THE SANTANA HEIR

by Elizabeth Lane

Grace wants to adopt her late sister's son. Peruvian
bachelor Emilio wants his brother's heir…and he wants
Grace in his bed. Can this bargaining-chip baby make
them a *real* family?

Look for the latest book in the scandalous
Billionaires and Babies miniseries next month!

Available wherever books and ebooks are sold.

HD73254